# THE BLACKOUT MURDERS

# THE BLACKOUT MURDERS

## Leo Kessler

This first world edition published in Great Britain 2004 by
SEVERN HOUSE PUBLISHERS LTD of
9–15 High Street, Sutton, Surrey SM1 1DF.
This first world edition published in the USA 2004 by
SEVERN HOUSE PUBLISHERS INC of
595 Madison Avenue, New York, N.Y. 10022.

British Library Cataloguing in Publication Data

Kessler, Leo, 1926-
  The blackout murders
  1.  Serial murder investigation - England - London - Fiction
  2.  Serial murderers - England - London - Fiction
  3.  World War, 1939-1945 - England - London - Fiction
  4.  War stories
  I.  Title
  823.9'14 [F]

  ISBN 0-7278-6063-1

Except where actual historical events and characters are being
described for the storyline of this novel, all situations in this
publication are fictitious and any resemblance to living persons
is purely coincidental.

Typeset by Palimpsest Book Production Ltd.,
Polmont, Stirlingshire, Scotland.
Printed and bound in Great Britain by
MPG Books Ltd., Bodmin, Cornwall.

For Gill, who made it possible – and enjoyable.

*L. Kessler.*

# Note by Col. R. Mackenzie, Intelligence Corps (Retd)

The summer of 1942 marked the nadir of British hopes in WWII. The British Army had suffered defeat after defeat. Much of the British Empire in the East had been lost. Admittedly we had gained two new allies after our eighteen-month-long lone fight against the enemy: Russia and the United States of America. But Russia was fighting for its life by July 1942 and the USA had just about managed to scrape together two divisions of green troops to send to the UK. Our one attempt to take the offensive to the German enemy at Dieppe that summer ended in a bloody defeat.

At home the bomb-scarred streets of our capital, London, were abruptly gripped by a new wave of terror. But it didn't come from the Germans. It came from our own kind. A killer was on the loose in London's blacked-out streets: one who sparked off the biggest manhunt since the days of the infamous Jack the Ripper.

Then the grisly, politically highly explosive story of this 'Khaki Ripper', as he was called by the frightened citizens of the nation's capital, could not be told. If it had been, it might have caused a tremendous blow to Anglo-American relations. Now it can be, sixty years or so on. It isn't a pleasant tale. But then in those days, gentle reader, there were no pleasant tales, were there?

*R. Mackenzie, DSO, MC, Cheltenham, England, Summer 2003.*

# Prelude to a Horror

# One

## Whistles Shrilled the Alarm

R ight on cue, the three Beaufighters howled in straight from the sea. They had already reached 300 mph. Their prop wash churned the grey-green water into a wild fury. Brazen lights sparkled the length of the fighters' stubby wings. Instinctively the little group of Anglo-American observers on the clifftop ducked in alarm. The fighters came closer. The pilots were flying so low that it seemed they couldn't avoid disaster – come smashing into the earth. But the RAF pilots were experts at this deadly business; didn't they hit real targets on the other side of the Channel every day?

Now like angry red hornets their shells raced towards the line of earthen bunkers which were the 'enemy'. Smoke rose immediately. Logs splintered like matchwood. Grass sods and bits and pieces of corrugated iron flew into the air. In an instant all was chaos and confusion.

Now out of the billowing white smokescreen spread by the destroyers scuttling back and forth, the first blunt-nosed barges began to emerge. Immediately the 'enemy' gunners dug in further down the cliff took up the challenge. Abruptly the spring landscape was full of the angry snap-and-crackle of small-arms fire. Like angry woodpeckers, heavy Vickers machine guns joined in. All around the slow-moving steel barges, packed with troops, the sea erupted in vicious little white-capped spurts. Now there was the clang of steel hitting steel; the howl of a slug ricochetting off the barges' sides. Braving the 'enemy' fire, for the 'enemy' were using live bullets and not the blanks the attackers had been used to so far, one of the attackers popped his head up over the side of a barge and snapped off a couple of wild shots at the dug-in 'enemy'.

With a harsh grinding of wet, gleaming shingle, the first barge came to an abrupt halt on the little beach. A clang of steel. A rattle of rusty chains. Its front flap slapped the shingle. Inside, the men waiting for this moment wasted no time. Soon they'd be doing this for real. Their lives might well depend upon how smartly they got off the beach. They pelted to left and right, their bodies crouched, rifles and other weapons held in front of them at the port, eyes wide and wild, as if this was the real thing and at any moment a burst of angry machine-gun fire could cut them to pieces.

Now barge after barge began hitting the beach. More and more Rangers swarmed out of them, running for all they were worth, automatically spreading out to both flanks.

Further up the beach, the first of the Rangers had halted momentarily at the base of the steep chalk cliffs. Round the gunners armed with the rocket launchers, the others had formed a defensive perimeter. Above them another flight of Beaufighters raced by at a tremendous speed, dragging their shadows behind them like those great evil black hawks, harbingers of sudden violent death.

'*Fire!*' a hoarse gasping voice ordered.

A soft belch. A puff of brilliant white smoke. The smoke cloud burst. Out of its centre snaked a length of rope, attached to a gleaming steel grapnel. It hurtled towards the clifftop. Behind it the rope zig-zagged rapidly towards the target. *Whack!* The steel hook slapped into the rock. The gunners pulled hard, faces lathered in sweat as if greased by vaseline. The prongs grated against the stone. But the grapnel held.

The Rangers wasted no more time. As more and more of the rope grapnels shot upwards, they grabbed the ropes and pulled them taut. Next instant they were swarming up them like olive-drab monkeys. All around them bullets slammed into the chalk cliff. They were showered with bits of stone. They didn't seem to notice; panting frantically like ancient asthmatics in the throes of final attack they kept going doggedly.

Then it happened. Just as the first batch of Rangers reached the top and paused there an instant before clambering over the edge, there was a shrill, hysterical scream like that of a woman seized by abject fear. To the left a young Ranger, his face contorted by utter overwhelming terror, tried to hold on to his rope, blood spurting from a great wound in his side in a scarlet arc. To no avail! Next moment, his arms flailing wildly, trailing his final scream behind, he fell to the beach far below. He slammed into the shingle with such force that his body split. An instant later he died there in a star of his own bright-red blood.

Someone shrilled a whistle. Another followed. The observers looked aghast. Here and there a British umpire waved his flag. Whether to stop the exercise or insist it should continue, no one knew. For it was clear that Ranger trainees, all picked, big and powerful young men, were suddenly scared. It was one of those moments that experienced trainers or commanders in the field fear: men going to ground and the possibility that they might not get up again, or could even run away.

Colonel Lucien Truscott, the new head of the US Rangers here in Britain, flamboyant ex-cavalryman in his riding boots, white breeches and leather jacket, moaned aloud. 'Sweet Jesus,' he cried, as for a moment or two the 'enemy' guns fell silent, 'the young buggers are going to ground.' He looked at the Commando major, who was in charge of the Rangers' training. 'What the Sam Hill does a guy do in a situation like this?'

Truscott need not have worried. A British officer in shabby khaki with stocking cap covering his unruly bright-red hair detached himself from the observation group. Ignoring the lone Bren gun that was still peppering the stalled men on the clifftop with tracer, firing to both flanks in a lethal morse, he ran towards them.

*'Lieutenant O'Corrigan!'* the Commando major cried urgently. 'Get down for God's sake man . . .' His face flushed an angry purple. 'I order you . . .' The words died on his thin cruel lips. O'Corrigan wasn't listening. He was pelting towards the stalled Americans, arms working like pistons, the tracer digging up spouts of earth all around his flying heels, as if the Bren gunner had gone mad and thought the running man was a real enemy.

O'Corrigan skidded to a stop. His chest heaving with the effort of running all out, he stood hands on his hips in front of the frightened Rangers and gasped. 'All right, you sad sacks of Yankee shite . . . on your feet! You want to become Rangers . . . Commandos . . . All right, you pregnant penguins, show me you're worthy of the title . . . Off to the assault course!' For one long moment they appeared not to be going to move and then they were on their feet taunted all the time by the crazy Irishman, who was already half drunk this spring morning. Next moment they were off.

Spread out at five yards' intervals, they ran forward, firing from the hip as they ran. A line of concertina wire, six foot high, curled outwards and cruelly sharp. The Irishman didn't hesitate. He flung himself bodily at it, arms outstretched. It was as if he were launching himself

8

from a diving board. But there was no pleasure in this dive. He yelped as the cruel metal spikes tore into his body. But O'Corrigan knew what he was doing. 'On yer skates, Yanks!' he yelled above the maddening dangerous chatter of the Bren guns. 'Don't stand there like spare cocks at a wedding. *Move!*'

They moved. Remembering their training, one by one they clambered up the Irishman's body, using it as a bridge across the wire. Then they were over and, expertly, O'Corrigan somersaulted over the barbed wire behind them, landing lightly on the tips of his toes like a trained athlete.

'Holy shit!' Truscott exclaimed in delight to the Commando major. 'That officer of yours is first class. He's a guy I'd like to take into combat with me once my Rangers are trained.'

The Commando major mumbled something, but whatever he said, his tone didn't sound very complimentary. Truscott didn't notice. He was too enthralled by the young Commando officer, who had apparently taken over and was leading these reluctant heroes through the assault course, although he was risking his own life doing so. The gunners acting as the 'enemy' were still using live ammunition and as always casualties up to 10 per cent were expected during these live-fire exercises; they were however supposed to come from the trainees *not* their trainers.

Now the Rangers were crawling up a muddy slope criss-crossed by knee-high barbed wire. Hosepipes had turned the slope into a glistening, treacherous morass. Time and time again the men slipped or they caught their packs on the barbed wire above them. The slope was loud with the curses of the Rangers, ripping their flesh cruelly on the barbs, as thunderflashes exploded on all sides and the white blur of tracer hissed through the air just above their helmeted heads.

But still the Irishman would brook no submission or surrender to the terrain. He cajoled, praised, cursed the mud-smeared Rangers, crying over and over again, 'Come on you Yank bastards, let's see some life from you! You ain't in the frigging PX now, buying chocolate bars – this is the real stuff . . . *Move it, willya, or yer'll have my boot up yer fat yankee arses . . . M . . . O . . . V . . . E!'*

The Commando major tut-tutted at such crude language, but Truscott slapped his leather riding crop against the side of his highly polished riding boot, exclaiming, 'That's the stuff to give the troops, Major. Makes 'em realize that this is the real war . . . where guys get killed dead. Attaboy, Lootenant!'

Now they were up the slope. Up in front of them was a high brick wall. Soaked and mud-stained, the Rangers, gasping fervently, staggered towards it, still urged on by O'Corrigan. 'Come on,' he urged them. 'Get up and over . . . *Do it!* Too much five against one in yer bunks at night, I wager.' He rushed forward through the brown choking smoke that was now being released over the 'battlefield' and caught one of the laggards a tremendous kick in the rear so that he went full length in the mud. The Commando major groaned with embarrassment. Truscott laughed out loud. But not for long now.

'*TANKS!*' one of the umpires bellowed through his megaphone to warn the Rangers. 'Tanks on the left flank . . . Prepare to repel armour.'

O'Corrigan reacted immediately. 'Into yer holes!' he cried over the rusty rumble of tracks emerging out of the smokescreen. 'Come on. Shift it . . . Into those holes or they'll be turning you lot into one of yer Hamburgers that yer like scoffing!'

They needed no urging. As the Bren-gun carriers which represented 'enemy' armour came heading towards the Rangers in a steel 'V', churning up earth and pebbles behind them in a furious wake, the American trainees flung themselves into the already prepared slit trenches. Watching next to Colonel Truscott, the Commando major clenched his fist till it hurt. He had never liked this part of the beach assault exercise even when he was leading trained Commandos. One wrong move, a moment of panic, and the trainee might well be crushed into a bloody pulp by those churning tracks. O'Corrigan didn't seem to care. He stood there alone, red hair glistening in the first rays of the sun, face stubborn, defiant, even wilful, like a man who was prepared to challenge fate.

Now the little armoured vehicles were swinging to left and right. O'Corrigan swung his head back and forth, as if ascertaining they were holding their true course; for he, too, naturally knew the deadly dangers of this terrible manoeuvre. Then they were rolling right over the tops of the slit trenches, slipping and sliding; while below, crouched in a foetal position, the young Americans screamed in sudden panic, their nostrils filled with the stench of petrol, hot oil dripping on to them, each praying fervently that the sides of their particular hole wouldn't crumple and lead to the inevitable disaster. Then they were gone and the Commando major was breathing a sigh of relief as head after head popped up from the holes like those of rabbits. No one had been hurt this time.

'Final phase, gentlemen!' the chief umpire yelled through his megaphone as O'Corrigan rallied his rattled troops, yelling insults and encouragements at them, as they clambered reluctantly out of their holes. 'Assault on enemy gun battery at three o'clock . . . to the right of that clump of yellow gorse.'

Obediently Truscott and the other observers, British and American, swung their glasses round to view the spot indicated. 'The troops will attack at the double. There will be tracer crossfire from each end of the skirmish line, some ten yards off the advance . . . As long as the men keep moving in an orderly fashion, there'll be no casualties. Everything will go to plan . . . Closest we can get to the real thing, Colonel Truscott, sir.'

Happily the new Ranger chief yelled back. 'Holy shit, I'd not like to get any frigging closer!' He smiled happily at the Commando major, who looked as worried as ever as he watched O'Corrigan, the crazy Mick, preparing to lead the Rangers' mock attack.

The Rangers formed up. They were wild-eyed, filthy now and dripping with sweat. They had been considered America's elite, as Truscott had picked them individually to become the United States Army's equivalent of the British Commandos, but not one of them had imagined even in their wildest dreams that their training could be as hard, as dangerous, as this. They had already suffered 10 per cent casualties. Now they considered they'd be lucky if they survived the rest of this morning without further injury.

O'Corrigan did not seem even to care. He showed not the least sign of fear, even of hesitation, as the two marksmen at the flanks opened up with their Bren guns, forming a white, hissing 'V' of tracer a handful of yards in front of the skirmish line. 'Forward!' he cried.

Hesitantly they began their advance towards the 'enemy gun position'. They walked slowly, even ponderously, like farm labourers returning home after a long hard day in their fields. Bullets ripped up the turf just in front of them. 'Shorts' dropped at their feet. To their front the white tracer sliced the sky like lethal morse. Some maintained later the 'limey slugs' had been so close they could feel the heat of the bullets on their faces.

Then it happened. A bullet howled off a concealed rock in the turf. It shot upwards. A Ranger yelled in pain. His Garand fell from his suddenly nerveless fingers. He faltered to a halt. Slowly, very slowly, as if seen in slow motion, something grey, hideous and steaming started to crawl like a deadly snake from his shattered red gore of guts. Next moment he fell to the ground, writhing and howling pitifully like some wild animal caught in a trap.

'God Almighty!' Truscott exclaimed. 'The poor bastard's bought it.'

The Commando major frowned, but said nothing. Orders had come from the very top to treat these first American soldiers to go into action in this year of 1942 with kid gloves. Now they'd had their first fatalities of the war, killed by an ally, British soldiers. Hell's bells, he told himself with a sinking feeling, there was going to be a stink about this. He only hoped he wouldn't have to take the can back; he had his career in the Regular Army to think about.

That deadly shot had its effect. The Rangers faltered to a stop. Here and there the more fearful dropped to the ground, hugging the earth, with their hands pressed hard over their ears like scared children trying to drown out the sound they dreaded.

O'Corrigan's narrow Irish face flushed an angry scarlet. Ignoring the tracer zipping furiously to left and right, he bellowed, beside himself with rage. 'Get on your frigging feet this instant!' he yelled above the chatter of the light machine guns. 'Do you hear? *On your feet!* By God, if you're not on yer frigging feet in half a second, there'll be trouble.' He kicked the nearest Ranger hard in the ribs. The man didn't seem to notice; he was too scared.

13

For a moment, the Commando officer didn't seem to know what to do. But Truscott, observing him through his field glasses, could see his chest heaving to and fro rapidly, as if he were trying to control himself by sheer naked will power. Next to him the Commando major, knowing his career stood on a knife's edge, willed the hot-headed Irishman not to do anything foolish, knowing at the same time the damned Mick would.

O'Corrigan did. He cried, 'Will you buggers never move?' The anger in his voice all too clear. Focusing his field glasses, the Commando major stared at O'Corrigan's hard, handsome, bitter face, the lips drooping a little in the corners like those of a man who had been disappointed in life. But there was no mistaking the purpose and determination stamped on those hard features. It was the face of a man born to command and lead – and die young.

The Rangers still refused to move. They hugged the earth like a lover. O'Corrigan lost his patience altogether. 'Bad cess on ye!' he yelled and reached into the khaki haversack slung across his broad chest. From it he pulled one of the training hand grenades. They weren't so powerful as the standard British Army No 36 grenade. But they were live and could be deadly at close quarters. In his rage O'Corrigan didn't concern himself with the inherent dangers of his action now.

The watching Commando major looked aghast as O'Corrigan put the deadly little steel egg to his lips. 'Oh my God—' he exclaimed, realizing what the crazy Mick was about to do, the words dying on his lips, as O'Corrigan tugged out the cotter pin with his teeth.

Next to him Colonel Truscott asked, 'Is that a live grenade—?' The rest of his question was drowned by the roar of the bomb exploding. It did so some ten yards behind the reluctant Americans. In a ball of angry yellow-red flame, it detonated, sending razor-sharp gleaming shards of steel hissing through the air. O'Corrigan ignored the danger from fragments. He cried, 'Up, yer damned young fools . . . Ye'll be sitting ducks on the frigging day . . . *Move!*'

The bold gesture worked. In an instant the reluctant heroes of a second before sprang to their feet. 'That's the ticket, me boyos,' O'Corrigan cried exuberantly. Whooping crazily like a bunch of drunken Red Indians, the Rangers charged the 'enemy' gun pit.

Colonel Truscott breathed out hard and wiped the sweat off his brow with the white silk muffler which he affected. 'Holy cow, what a soldier! Never seen anything like that. Tossing a grenade at your soldiers. Some guy!'

Next to him, the Commando major showed less enthusiasm for Rory O'Corrigan, MC and Bar, veteran of France, Greece, the Western Desert. For, lying prone on the smoke-charred turf as the other Rangers took the hilltop position, lay the still body of one of their comrades who had not risen to take part in that wild assault; and somehow the fearful Commando major felt that that particular Yank would never rise again.

# Two

O utside the Commando troop office the bugle sounded
sweet, clear, even haunting. It was followed almost
instantly by the harsh crunch of hobnailed boots on the
gravel that lined the path leading to the office. Standing
near the door the young officer, capped, belted and wearing
a .38 revolver in the blancoed holster at his right hip, said
in an embarrassed sort of a way, 'Lieutenant O'Corrigan,
would you mind rising? I think they're about ready for you.
That sounds like your escort.'

O'Corrigan, still astonished by what had happened to
him in the last forty-eight hours, gave the callow subaltern
a smile, though those dark blue eyes of his didn't light
up. For, puzzled as he was, he realized, as he had said
to himself nearly every hour since the Commando brigade
major had had him placed under close arrest, *You've fucked
up for good this time, Rory, me boyo. They've got you by
the short and curlies at last.* Aloud he said, 'Are you going
to be the prisoner's friend as well?' He meant the officer
who defended a prisoner at a court martial.

The young officer opposite him actually blushed. 'I'm
afraid I am, O'Corrigan.'

The red-haired Irishman managed a wintry smile. 'I'm
sure, lad, you'll do your best for me.'

'But I've never done anything like this before, O'Corrigan,'
the other man protested. 'And I'll be faced by a trained

16

lawyer from the Judge Advocate's Branch and the case isn't just about going AWOL for a couple of days.' The young subaltern stopped abruptly as if he had suddenly realized the import of what he was saying; he was about to defend a fellow officer who could be sent to jail for years if he was found guilty.

'Cheer up, lad. There's worse things at sea,' O'Corrigan said, as the door was flung open and a hard-faced captain of the Military Police came pushing his way in, gimlet eyes beneath the stiff peak of his immaculate cap suspicious, as if the two young officers were up to doing something they shouldn't be. 'Prisoner!' he snapped, 'Off with your belt.' He didn't wait to see if the prisoner complied with his order. Instead he continued with a harsh 'Stand up!' and without turning his head, he barked, 'Escort stand by to take the prisoner!' Behind him the two gigantic Military Police corporals stamped their feet down mightily, as if they were trying to break through the floorboards.

A minute later and O'Corrigan was double-timing into the brigade HQ, being hurried along by the big MP officer, barking at him, 'Come on now, swing them arms . . .'

Under his breath the red-haired prisoner told the captain to do something sexual to himself that was physically impossible and then reacted automatically, as the MP barked, 'Prisoner and escort – *mark time!*' For what seemed an age, O'Corrigan and the two corporals marked time where they stood, knees moving up and down with rigid precision, stamping on the stone flags so that the whole place echoed with the noise of those heavy, hobnailed ammunition boots. O'Corrigan knew that the MP captain was making him sweat it out. It didn't worry him. He knew the whole procedure was traditionally used to awe, cow and intimidate the prisoner. It didn't have that effect on him. Indeed he was too angry at the whole bloody business, especially these MPs playing toy soldiers, to feel threatened. At that moment he would have gladly tossed another grenade under the lot of them. But that wasn't to be. For the time being the military establishment had him in its power, but as he promised himself grimly, as the doors of the court were opened, 'The buggers won't keep you long, Rory, old lad, come what may.'

The court consisted of three middle-aged officers, including a bald-headed brigadier from the Royal Army Service Corps, who was trying to look severe, but who was in reality really bored. Then there was his flustered and very unhappy young subaltern, acting as the 'prisoner's friend'. Opposite him was a lieutenant-colonel, swarthy and wearing gold-rimmed glasses, who kept touching his bald pate delicately, as if he were hoping to find evidence that his hair was beginning to grow. He'd be a trained lawyer from the Judge Advocate's Branch, and he had that self-satisfied cunning look about him, as if nothing had ever gone wrong in his life and never would.

At that moment O'Corrigan could imagine his defender's feelings. A very junior second lieutenant faced by a lieutenant-colonel, who outranked him in both training and several grades.

For a few moments a heavy silence, broken only by the subdued noises from outside, hung over the court. O'Corrigan knew it, too, was part of the treatment, intended to make the prisoner feel uneasy, even alarmed. But again it only served to increase the red-headed Irishman's contempt and anger.

These men, who were trying to break his spirit, were those who spoke the same language as he did, wore the same uniform, were supposedly fighting the same enemy. Yet the looks on their well-fed faces told him that *he* was the enemy at the moment. They hated him more than they

did the Germans. Why? Because they knew he was a
threat to their own security and their lazy amateurish
way of running the war. He had attempted to show the
men entrusted to his care the cruel realities of combat; but
they and their kind hadn't liked that. And they were going
to punish him for it. Today they were going to break him
once and for all. But at the back of his mind a hard little
voice intoned, 'Not if I have my fucking way!'

'Prisoner –' it was the colonel from the Judge Advocate's Branch, a slimy, superior, even supercilious tone
to his voice – 'tell the court your name, rank, unit and
current appointment at the time of your arrest . . . er,
please.' Even as he remembered that he was addressing
a fellow officer, who had not been tried yet, so he knew
he had to use the word 'please' as a matter of courtesy,
he glanced across at the brigadier with a knowing look,
as if to say, '*We won't have to say "please" to the cocky
bugger much longer, sir.*'

O'Corrigan did as he was requested, his gaze fixed on
the distant horizon behind the prosecutor's back.

The prosecutor said, 'These are the charges against the
prisoner.' He looked at the pad in his hand, though he
knew the charges already by heart. 'One, he failed to
take comprehensive safety measures in the training of a
group of our American allies. Two, he vented his rage
on them when, although they were only trainees, perhaps
not fully cognizant of British Army training methods, they
didn't press home their assault during an exercise.' He
paused, as if he were now to make a significant point,
gazing around the court as he did so, until his gaze,
full of theatrical gravitas, came to rest on O'Corrigan.
'Three, he lost his temper completely, as he has been
known to do before, and flung a live grenade at the
Americans. This resulted, I am afraid to say, in the death

of one American soldier and the wounding of another.' He
sat down.

The brigadier came to life, as if he had been dozing with
his eyes open. He looked at the pink-cheeked subaltern,
who the year before had still been at his public school,
and asked, 'How does the prisoner plead?'

'Not guilty as charged, sir,' the unfortunate officer
stuttered.

The brigadier looked at the 'prisoner's friend', who was
beginning to blush furiously again as if he had just realized
he had forgotten to put on his trousers. 'As charged . . .
What's that supposed to mean?' he snapped testily.

'Well, sir.' The subaltern looked up at the ceiling, as if
he half hoped he'd get an immediate message from heaven,
giving him guidance. But there was no divine assistance
forthcoming.

'Come on, man, get on with it, Lieutenant!'

Well, sir, the prisoner admits he threw the grenade. But
he didn't do it in order to injure or kill these American –
er – Rangers—'

'I shall not plead, Brigadier,' O'Corrigan's voice cut in
harshly.

The brigadier's gaze clicked in O'Corrigan's direction.
'What did you say?'

O'Corrigan repeated his statement, adding stonily, 'All
I'll say is this. I did what I did in order to save those men's
lives when they go into action. I did it to end this bloody
war quickly, as *trained* men will and untrained won't –
they'll simply throw their lives away for no purpose.
I did it because I can't stand any longer the kind of
nine-o'clock-to-five-o'clock battle, with an hour off for
lunch, that you gentlemen wish to conduct, that is, those
of you who will ever venture to the front . . .'

'Stop this . . . do you hear what I say?' the brigadier

cried, springing red-faced to his feet and slamming his cane down on the blanket-covered trestle table in front of him. 'I will not have this kind of seditious nonsense in my court. Stop this at once!'

The MP captain grabbed O'Corrigan's arm; opposite, the smooth lawyer-colonel smirked, as if he knew that O'Corrigan had lost his case already due to his outburst, while the brigadier pulled out a silk khaki handkerchief from his sleeve and started to mop his brow angrily.

In that moment of high drama, the only one who seemed to retain his composure was the prisoner himself. He had said his piece; he had got his resentment off his chest. That resentment had been building up ever since he had been wounded in yet another failed British attack in North Africa and had decided to volunteer from hospital for the new Commandos in the hope of seeing some real action, where he could use his battle skills, only to find that the Commando brigade was as set in its ways as the rest of the British Home Army was.

But the brigadier was determined to go through with the proceedings, although he had already decided in his own mind that the damned Irishman, O'Corrigan was true to his type. He'd give him the maximum sentence possible. Those damned Micks were a bloody nuisance; they should never have allowed them to join the British Army. They simply had no idea of how to behave as soldiers, even Churchill's new blue-eyed boy, that Montgomery fellow, a cad if he had ever seen one.

So, while O'Corrigan stood there stony-faced, his gaze revealing nothing and his boyish 'prisoner's friend' stuttered and faltered his way through the proceedings, the trial ran its course. First the Commando major was called. His evidence was as O'Corrigan expected it would be – prejudiced. He hadn't wanted O'Corrigan in the training brigade. The Irishman's record showed him to be bolshy. He was not the kind of officer that he, the brigade major, wanted to train Commandos, who were inclined to be ill-disciplined as it was.

It was the kind of evidence that both the brigadier and the man from the Judge Advocate's office wanted. Both of them thanked the officer for his 'objective and precise appraisal'. It was no use the 'prisoner's friend' attempting to show that O'Corrigan had volunteered for the Commando from his sickbed in an attempt to get back into action as soon as possible. The brigadier more or less told the young subaltern to shut up.

The next witness the defence produced was no less a person than Colonel Truscott, the American head of the new Rangers. He was dressed as flamboyantly as ever, and the brigadier frowned with distaste as he entered the little country room with a swagger and a creak of his cavalryman's riding boots. For a moment or two O'Corrigan felt a flicker of hope as Truscott seemed to show some understanding of his position as a man training young men to go into combat. He said, 'It is my contention that it is better to train hard and fight easy. It is better than the other way round. Now in the case of Lieutenant O'Corrigan here, I feel—'

'With all due respect, Colonel, your feelings are not relevant in this courtroom,' the Judge Advocate's representative cut him off sharply. The lawyer knew from the look of disdain on the brigadier's face that he had the court on his side. It was clear that the brigadier had taken an instant dislike to the Yankee colonel. He felt he was on safe ground giving the latter a hard time.

Truscott looked both angry and confused. 'Well,' he demanded, 'what do you expect me to say?'

'This. You are our new ally here and you deserve to

have every respect paid to you and your men, sir. After
all, you have travelled three thousand miles to come and
fight. And what do we do? Or in this case, the prisoner?'
He spread his hands out expressively. 'We attempt to kill
your men. Yessir!' He raised his voice melodramatically
before Truscott could object, as he seemed about to. 'That's
it in a nutshell. The prisoner wasn't just trying to *train* your
men and make them ready for war, he was, for reasons,
God knows, clear only to himself, trying to *kill* them!'

Colonel Truscott had left the court in a confused mood.
He had taken a quick look at O'Corrigan, as if he were
seeing him for the very first time and was wondering
urgently if he had misjudged him totally when he had
praised his leadership qualities on the day of the grenade
incident.

Even as he passed, O'Corrigan knew his fate was sealed.
But it was the last witness who really turned the knife in the
wound, as far as O'Corrigan was concerned. Dramatically
enough he was wheeled into the court by an orderly of
the Royal Army Medical Corps, who was equipped with
a small bottle of oxygen, as if ready to administer it at a
moment's notice to the big blond youngster in the chair,
his legs covered with a rug, as if he had incurred serious
injury to them.

O'Corrigan knew him well enough, as the court heard
his name and rank and the other relevant details. 'Swede',
his comrades in the Rangers called him. 'Swede Larsen', a
big lumbering handsome farm boy from Minnesota, blond
and curly-haired, so that the girls in the Commando NAAFI
idolized him and drooled on about how the American
looked like 'one o' them Hollywood film stars'.

Swede knew it too, and his general effect on the local
women. He'd look at his big powerful hands like steam
shovels, as he'd lie naked on his bunk after duty, toying

23

idly with his penis, boasting, 'Everything's big about us Minnesota boys – big head, big hands and, as you guys can see, a real big peter, as well as.' And he'd flip up his penis, a broad smile on his handsome face, so that his comrades could get a clear look at the organ. 'Yessir, when Swede Larsen's had 'em, it's no use any other guy having a go. The broads ain't just interested.' And he'd give his penis another jerk so that it stood immediately like a policeman's truncheon.

O'Corrigan hadn't liked him from the start and had had occasion a couple of times to reprimand him for his behaviour on and off duty. But Larsen had another, totally different side to him, O'Corrigan realized. Once, just after the Rangers had arrived at the remote Commando camp for training, he had been the orderly officer, doing the usual midnight round, accompanied by Sergeant Hawkins, the orderly sergeant.

As was customary, the two of them prowled the sleeping Nissen-hut camp, merely exchanging a few low words, ensuring that the sentries were not sleeping at their posts or having a sly 'spit and a draw', giving their positions away with the glowing end of their cigarette. It was not that O'Corrigan was one of those orderly officers who liked to catch private soldiers out and took pleasure in putting them on a charge. He was intent on drilling into these future combat soldiers that even little things like having a forbidden smoke might well cost them their lives in the front line.

But it had not been someone having a fly 'spit and a draw' that had attracted the two of them to the Nissen hut which served as the troop's ablutions and lavatory hut – 'the bogs', as the trainees called the smelly tin-roofed structure. It had been a kind of weird moaning and wailing, which Sergeant Hawkins, a veteran of India and Egypt before the war, had maintained later, reminded him 'of one of them wog wallahs kicking up a racket at a funeral. Send the shivers down my spine'.

It hadn't sent the shivers down O'Corrigan's spine. He was far too unimaginative for that. But it had made him eager to investigate the strange moaning and wailing. Adjusting his orderly officer's armband more tightly, as if he might need the authority the armband conferred upon him, he whispered urgently. 'Come on, Hawkins, let's have a dekko.'

By the spectral light of the half moon scudding in and out of the silver clouds, they advanced almost noiselessly upon the Nissen hut from which the strange sounds were coming. Carefully Hawkins opened the door to be greeted by the usual stink that came from the ablutions hut. But this night he didn't notice the smell. For his gaze was caught immediately by the totally naked figure kneeling on the sodden duckboards that ran the length of the place, hands raised as if in prayer or supplication, muttering, 'Praise be the Lord for His nightly acts . . . praise be God for His excellent greatness . . . praise Him with the soul of the trumpet.'

'Bloody hell!' Hawkins exclaimed, hand falling instinctively to the holster of his revolver, feeling at the same time the small hairs at the back of his neck grow erect with shock. 'What the frig—?'

'Shut up!' O'Corrigan hissed. Once as a boy in Ireland he had been a devout Catholic until the Jesuits had knocked religion out of him. All the same, he recognized the psalm and felt that he should not come between a man and his religion, even one as nasty, brutal and lecherous as PFC Larsen.

'But he's bloody barmy, sir,' Hawkins had objected *sotto voce*.

'Never mind,' O'Corrigan whispered. 'Let's leave him to do it. He's doing no harm.'

But it was only later when they were drinking cocoa with the sergeant of the guard in the snug atmosphere of the guardroom with the off-duty sentries, clad in their overcoats and boots, snoring in their bunks on either side that Hawkins said plaintively, 'But the Yankee bloke must have done some harm to hissen or somebody, sir.'

'How do you mean, Hawkins?' O'Corrigan had asked, lifting his frozen face from the comforting hot steam of the cocoa.

''Cos, sir, his right hand – I could see it distinctly in the moonlight, was dripping with blood.'

Next morning when O'Corrigan had taken the Rangers out for a twenty-mile speed march, he had made a special point of looking at the big handsome American's hands. But there had not been the slightest scratch on them. Thereafter, he had forgotten all about the matter, though he somehow suspected that from then onwards, PFC Larsen had begun watching him with a certain wariness. Why, O'Corrigan hadn't the slightest idea. Now, however, Larsen had turned up at his court martial in the guise of a seriously hurt man, complete with nurse and emergency bottle of oxygen. To what purpose?

# Three

'State your name, rank and appointment.' The Judge Advocate colonel commenced with the usual formula, after fussing with Larsen in his wheelchair, as if he were very concerned that the young American Ranger should suffer no further pain.

O'Corrigan looked on with a mixture of cynicism at the colonel's attempt, and wonder at the American's presence at his court martial. For the life of him he couldn't fathom why Larsen should be there save for the fact that he had been apparently wounded by that damned grenade he had thrown at the trainees to get them moving.

Larsen gave the required information in a low husky voice, head slightly bent and to one side, as if he were a man who was bravely facing up to some considerable pain – all for the sake of justice. *Arsehole!* Rory O'Corrigan told himself. The big Swedish-American had the strength of an ox; he was obviously putting it on.

'Now, Ranger, tell me exactly what you saw at the time of the incident with the grenade.'

'Yessir,' Larsen answered dutifully. 'Though I was a bit confused – after being hit.'

'Yes, we can understand that, Ranger,' the colonel said sympathetically while the brigadier from the Royal Army Service Corps nodded his understanding.

'Well, sir, we'd gone to ground. But it wouldn't have

27

taken more than a minute before our Top – I mean our top sergeant, Hutchinson – would have rallied us and got us moving again. He wasn't one to stand any nonsense from the troops.'

The brigadier leaned across the trestle table and snapped, as if he had made a very significant discovery. 'You mean, soldier, that this was only a temporary halt and that your own NCOs would have soon rallied you men.'

'Yessir,' Larsen agreed in that low, suffering voice he had adopted for the trial.

'Thank you,' the brigadier said and flashed a look at the officer from the Judge Advocate's Branch, who took up the point immediately; he'd understood the significance of that look.

'So, there was no need for any radical action to get the Rangers moving once more?'

'Yessir.'

'So can you tell the court why you think that Lieutenant O'Corrigan threw the grenade . . . ?'

'I'd like to object to that question, sir.' The 'prisoner's friend' attempted to defend his client. 'I don't think that it is a permissible question.'

The brigadier rapped his swagger stick across the table angrily. 'Of course it's a permissible question!' he barked. 'This man is a witness. He was there. His testimony to the events is vital.'

'But it's subjective testimony, sir,' the young subaltern said weakly, flushing brilliant red once more, while O'Corrigan told himself the lad hadn't a chance. The court had already made up its mind about his guilt.

'I can't say why he threw it, sir,' Larsen said slowly, as if he were considering the question very seriously. 'Except perhaps . . .' He hesitated and the colonel said eagerly, 'Go on, Ranger. Don't be afraid – say what you think.

We understand.' He leaned forward as if he physically wanted to push the witness into completing his sentence.

'That Lieutenant O'Corrigan didn't like us Americans very much.'

The colonel seized upon the statement like a terrier worrying a rat. 'You mean to say, PFC Larsen, that this was a personal matter?' he rasped urgently.

'Perhaps, sir.' Larsen kept his head low, so that O'Corrigan couldn't see his eyes. But he knew instinctively that the American Ranger was savouring this moment; he'd got him by the short and curlies, well and truly so. 'I heard Top Sergeant Hutchinson shout out that there was no need for the Lieutenant to do anything – he'd got the situation well in hand. Something like that. But Lieutenant O'Corrigan wasn't listening – I think. Just as I turned to see what was going on before I got to my feet and continued the attack with the rest, he threw the grenade right at the men in the rear. Poor Hutchinson—' He broke off with a sob, as if he were too overcome with emotion to continue, while the man from the Judge Advocate's Branch feigned compassion and understanding, knowing that this dramatic pause was more effective than a thousand words.

O'Corrigan couldn't contain himself any longer. 'Why, you lying bastard!' he yelled, his face as red as his hair. 'I did nothing of the sort. Nor did your sergeant say—'

The big MP captain slammed his stick down hard. 'Enough of that, prisoner!' he cried. Up at the trestle table, the brigadier joined in with 'You're not doing your case one bit of good by taking that—'

'*Fuck the case!*' O'Corrigan drowned the rest of his words and for the first time since Larsen had been wheeled into the court, he looked directly at the Irishman – and there was no mistaking that look of triumph in eyes that abruptly looked quite crazy.

O'Corrigan, however, had no time to consider why Larsen was doing what he was doing. He had been set up, he knew, and he was not going to tolerate being sent to prison by these bastards who were presiding over him. He took a deep breath. The MP captain seemed to realize what O'Corrigan was going to do. He jerked up his stick, as if to defend himself. Too late. O'Corrigan smashed his big fist right into the MP's stomach. He gasped and bent double, retching and fighting for air. O'Corrigan didn't give him a chance. As he did so, O'Corrigan brought up his right knee sharply in Commando style. It struck the MP on the point of the chin. The big MP went down as if poleaxed. He was unconscious before he hit the floor.

O'Corrigan sprang from the makeshift dock. Another MP, the bigger of the two corporals, tried to stop him. He hadn't a chance. O'Corrigan had long forgotten the Marquis of Queensbury rules. His right boot lashed out. The steel-tipped ammunition boot slammed into his shin. The MP yelped in agony. O'Corrigan pushed him – hard. He staggered into the other corporal. In a cursing, confused heap they went down together. Lightly, O'Corrigan sprang over the two MPs.

'*O'Corrigan!*' his 'prisoner's friend' gasped.

'Thanks all the same, old boy.'

O'Corrigan raced to where Larsen sat in his wheelchair. 'Bastard!' he snarled and with a quick jerk of his powerful wrists he overturned the contraption. Larsen fell cursing to the floor.

In an instant all was chaos, wild confusion, with the brigadier shouting off his head, puce-faced and hammering the table with his swagger stick. O'Corrigan grinned at him as he bolted for the door. 'Don't have a heart attack,' he gasped and, springing lightly over the guard commander's outstretched foot, ran for the camp exit. He didn't reach it. Little Sergeant Hawkins, the old sweat, appeared as if by magic. He thrust a key into O'Corrigan's hands. 'Fifteen-hundredweight van just round the corner, sir. Nicked it from the motor pool. Enough juice in the tank to get yer to the Big Smoke.' He meant London. 'God bless yer, sir. Best o' luck.'

'Thanks Hawkins.' Next moment O'Corrigan was running all out, arms working like pistons, while the camp's siren was sounding its dread warning. Five minutes later he was on the London road, overjoyed to find that the little sergeant had even removed the 'governor', which regulated the speed of Army vehicles. Within seconds he was driving all-out, going at more than sixty miles on hour now. His red Irish face creased in a tough grin. He was on his way. Where, he hadn't the faintest idea. All he knew was they'd never take him alive. Mrs Rory O'Corrigan's handsome son was not going to spend the rest of his born days in some damned English glasshouse. A few seconds later he had disappeared around the nearest bend, leaving the wail of the air-raid siren to die away behind him . . .

# Book One: Shadow of Jack the Ripper

'As women passed through the lightless streets at night they wondered whether the murderer might be lurking in wait for them.'
*Chief Supt F. Cherrill, Scotland Yard, 1942*

# One

'That's Pierrepoint, the Home Office's chief hangman,' Dalby explained in a whisper as he looked through the door of the observation chamber just behind the governor of Wandsworth Prison. The head of the Army's Special Intelligence Unit lowered his voice a little. 'He's to do the job.' Then like everyone else this dawn at Wandsworth Prison, his mood was subdued. Indeed, as Staff Sergeant Mackenzie, Major Dalby's assistant, told himself, the only one who didn't seem affected by the sombre mood of the place was the man who was to be hanged in the next half hour: the German spy, whom they had captured two days after he had parachuted into England in Hertfordshire. The German, held somewhere in a room off the execution chamber, waiting for Pierrepoint to ready him for that final 'drop', was singing lustily to himself about his 'nut-brown maiden' named Erika. Mackenzie, the German linguist told himself the spy would be the only one of the many score men and women executed here who would celebrate his impending death with a German folk song.

Still, he didn't feel very happy here, being present at the execution by hanging of a man they had apprehended and interrogated only a week ago, but Dalby had been adamant in that quiet but authoritarian manner of his. When Mackenzie had protested that there ought to be something they could do to save the German from the

*Leo Kessler*

hangman's rope – after all the German was really a soldier of another kind, fighting a lone battle behind enemy lines – 'No, Mac. Once that chap took off his uniformed parachute smock and helmet and walked out of his landing spot in civilian clothes, he was under sentence of death. We can't afford any weakness. The Hun won't attempt to invade us any more as he threatened to do back in 1940, but he is still beating us on virtually every front.' He had shaken his greying head sternly and finished with, 'Hardness is what England expects of us in 1942, strict bloody hardness!'

A few yards away in another room, the hangman was sizing up his victim. Pierrepoint was a big strong man himself, but the German spy towered above him. He had to be at least six foot three and he was burly with it. He'd have to work fast and trust in surprise to get the German's hands pinioned behind him so that he could be led to the gallows. The two prison officers, guarding the spy, would help. But they'd have to be nifty and use all their strength if there wasn't going to be a death-scene rumpus, which Pierrepoint, the Home Office's chief hangman, always thought was unprofessional.

The Catholic priest came in, a weedy fellow intoning his prayers in an Irish accent. Pierrepoint sniffed. He didn't hold with the Papists. Still, the presence of the priest might calm the prisoner, who was looking at the hangman challengingly, as if he was not prepared to be done to death quietly.

Pierrepoint decided it was time to move now. He moved forward, leather strap at the ready. The prisoner was quicker. He gave the priest a heavy shove. He went staggering to the wall. 'Hey, none of that,' the bigger of the two prison officers began. The spy slugged him in the mouth and shut off the rest of his protest. The guard went down on his knees, blood spurting in a bright red arc from his split mouth. Then the other guard swung his truncheon. It hit the spy at the side of his shaven head with a tremendous whack. He staggered but didn't seem to notice the hefty blow. He was coming straight at Pierrepoint now. The hangman dodged the rush. As the spy stumbled by him, the hangman grabbed his right wrist. In an instant he slapped the pinion strap around the wrist and tugged hard.

Normally Pierrepoint wouldn't have pulled the strap too tight. He thought it psychologically wrong to make the prisoner feel constricted or angry. This time he had no choice. The bull-like German was just too strong. He raised one big-booted foot and slapped it into the small of his back. With all his strength, he tugged and tugged until the strap was secure up to the second hole. Thus he, the hangman, and his victim started towards the scaffold and the waiting observers.

While Mackenzie watched in awe with the rest of them, Pierrepoint and his assistant, called Albert, swiftly completed the rest of that gruesome procedure, intended to send another human being to his death in a matter of seconds, for Pierrepoint prided himself on his split-second timing. As the spy stared at his captors, bulging-eyed and dangerous, the two hangmen strapped his feet. Then they placed the cap on his head and the hempen noose around the prisoner's neck.

Mackenzie caught his breath. This was it. Pierrepoint was now crossing to the lever, which would open the trap. In a second it would be all over. But in the same instant that the trap began to open, the spy took the initiative into his own hands. To everyone's horror, he jumped with his bound feet. Pierrepoint shouted. The noose was slipping. 'God Almighty!' he cried aloud. 'The poor bugger'll be choked to death!'

Hastily Mackenzie jerked away his gaze. But his boss, Dalby, continued to watch, his hand holding his unlit pipe totally steady, as if he was not one bit affected by what was taking place. Later, as they drank a whisky with the prison governor (though Pierrepoint had already departed with his five guineas back to his pub, Help the Poor Struggler) Dalby again made his standpoint quite clear. 'There can be no mercy with the enemy. There can be no mercy with anyone who helps the enemy.'

'But Major, do you think that death – the death penalty, I mean – stops that sort of thing?' Rather surprisingly the prison governor posed the question himself. 'In my experience, hanging such as we have just seen has never prevented a single murder. People continue to murder each other and I am sure the Hun will continue to find people prepared to come here and spy upon us, even if they know that they'll be confronted with the Pierrepoint family, who have been executing men – and women – since 1901.' The governor shrugged a little hopelessly like a man who had been tried too long and too often. 'What good does it all do?'

Major Dalby looked severely at the other man. 'That is not a proper attitude, Governor, if I may say so. We're living on a knife's edge in this country. We cannot afford to be soft, philosophize, question why we have to take life. If the British Empire is to survive, we must be hard, damned hard!'

Mackenzie told himself that as a young postgraduate student before the war he would have laughed out loud at such old-fashioned, reactionary thoughts, believing they were the kind of thing expressed by stuffy old colonels retired to Cheltenham. They were the attitudes of the past. Now he saw matters in a different light. Mackenzie frowned. 'But there is always some factor in a criminal's past, sir,' he objected mildly, 'or his background, to excuse him. There is a price for our passage through life, sir.' He was addressing his words to his boss and not to the prison governor and Dalby knew it. He answered, 'When you're young like you are, Mac, it is understandable that you think like that. But when you're old like me and know, perhaps, more about the human state, you will understand just how mistaken you were.' He forced a wintry smile and started to pick up his cane and cap. 'You'll learn, Mac. You'll bloody well learn all right.'

It was then that the chief warder knocked and came into the office, forgetting even to salute in his red-faced agitation. 'Sir . . . sir!' he stuttered urgently, 'There's been a terrible murder, sir.'

The governor looked at him and took his briar out of his mouth. 'And?' he queried.

'Just had a telephone call from the War Office, sir. Head of the Military Intelligence section.' He swallowed hard, as he recalled that only a minute before he had been standing at attention holding the phone, addressing a general for the first time in his life. 'He sez, sir, that these two officers should report to the War Office immediately.'

Dalby looked at the young staff sergeant and the question was clearly visible in his eyes. It was: *What in heaven's name have we from Special Intelligence got to do with a murder, terrible as it may be?*

Major Dalby was soon to be enlightened . . .

London looked shabbier than ever, Mackenzie told himself as the big staff car that the War Office had sent for them sped through the suburbs. Outside every food store and butcher's shop there were queues of women, carrying shopping baskets, their clothes poor, and with headscarves hiding their curlers. Here and there the young staff sergeant of Intelligence caught the notices painted on the windows of the butchers' shops proclaiming *Offal today – rations books H–M* and the like. Today it seemed housewives and mothers would stand in line for hours for a piece of pig's liver or a few pieces of tripe. Naturally chalked up on the bridges everywhere there was that new slogan, inspired by the communists eager to help their comrades in hard-pressed Soviet Russia, *Second Front 1942 – Now!*

Dalby saw the signs too and commented, a little wearily, 'Doubt if there'll be a second front in France even next year. We'll be lucky if we get one in 1944, Mac.'

'Yessir!' the younger man agreed. 'But the Yanks are coming.' He indicated the soldier lounging at the street corner, cap set at the back of his head, chewing gum steadily like a cow working on its cud.

Dalby nodded his agreement and commented, 'Yes, but when you think America's been at war nearly six months now and all they've managed to send to the UK in the way of troops is two divisions – and they're as inexperienced and as green as the growing corn. They certainly won't swing the balance in our favour against the Huns.'

'I suppose not, sir,' Mackenzie agreed, feeling suddenly overcome by a sense of despondency. The war had been going on for ever, it seemed. Now, it appeared, it would continue for years to come. It was all too bloody to contemplate. It was time to change the subject. 'About this girl, sir? What did they say at the War Office, if I may ask?'

'You may, though I can't tell you much. All I know is that a girl has been found in an air-raid shelter savagely murdered – an ATS to be exact.' Dalby meant a member of the Army's female auxiliary. 'And we've been ordered by the highest authority to look into it.'

'Highest authority, sir?' Mackenzie queried, surprised. 'The Chief of Intelligence?'

Dalby shook his head as the Humber staff car started to slow down. 'No, the chief of *everything*!'

'You mean . . . Mr Churchill, the PM?' Mackenzie gasped.

Dalby nodded solemnly and then tapped the army driver on the shoulder. 'Over there, Corporal . . . where that police car is standing.'

'Sir!' Obediently the driver changed down and brought the car to rest just outside the sandbagged air-raid shelter, where a couple of bobbies, middle-aged, carrying gas masks and helmets, were smoking somewhat hectically, as if they needed a smoke to soothe their nerves, Mackenzie couldn't help thinking.

Immediately they saw Dalby, they put out their cigarettes, snapped to attention and saluted. The bigger of the two said, 'The Chief Inspector's in there, sir . . . with the body.' Next to him the other policeman made a gulping noise at the mention of the body, as if he might begin vomiting at any moment. 'He's waiting for you, sir.'

Dalby touched his hand to his cap in acknowledgement, but he didn't enter the place immediately. Instead he surveyed it and the immediate surrounding area, while the two policemen watched him, obviously wondering what an army major had to do with this sordid murder.

The place was a typical brick-built surface shelter, with a few ripped sandbags piled up against its outer walls; there were hundreds of such shelters throughout London. Nowadays, since the great blitz of 1940–41 had ceased, such shelters were mostly used by tramps, usually deserters on the run, and courting couples.

Mackenzie, standing a little puzzled next to his chief, told himself that this particular one had been used a lot by the latter. There were used contraceptives everywhere near the door. A damned uncomfortable way of making love, he felt. Such places were usually damp, stank of cat's piss and provided, for the delights of sexual love, only a concrete bench running down one side from the blast-proof door. But still these days London was full of sex-starved soldiers and willing women, amateur and professional, who were prepared to copulate anywhere, as long as it brought pleasure or coins of the realm. Love and sex were in the very air of the capital.

Dalby cleared his throat. 'All right, let's go and have a look-see, Mac. The sooner we get to know what's going on, the better.' He pushed into the air-raid shelter and was immediately blinded by the glare of the light that the police had rigged up at the end of the shelter, for as always someone had stolen the bulb from the place's electric light; in 1942 electric bulbs were like gold.

There were two middle-aged men in the shelter, one with a Gladstone bag open next to him, kneeling over what appeared to be a bundle of wet khaki in the corner; the other turning to meet them, already aware of their presence.

He was tall, shaven-headed, dressed in a dark overcoat that had seen better days, puffing hard at the stump of a cigarette clasped in the corner of his wide cynical mouth. 'Major Dalby and Staff Sergeant Mackenzie.'

Dalby nodded.

'Chief Superintendent Fred Cherrill,' the policeman said. 'Everyone here calls me "Super". I won't shake your hand, Major. You don't know where it's been. I do.' He nodded grimly at the shape in the corner.

Dalby frowned and muttered something, while Mackenzie, with a young man's curiosity, tried to get a better view of what lay there. But the doctor's bulk, for he was certain the man with the Gladstone bag was a medic, prevented him from doing so.

'I don't know what the Army's got to do with this nasty

business, Major,' the Super went on, 'but I have been ordered to give you the fullest assistance by the assistant commissioner at the Yard.'

There it was again, Mackenzie told himself. Why was this obviously sordid little case exercising the minds of the great, he asked himself once more. And why had Special Intelligence been called in? There were a lot of questions, with, so far, no answers. He tensed and waited for explanations.

But the Super, in the manner of the traditional flatfoot, was obviously not going to be hurried. 'The body,' the policeman began, 'was discovered by a special constable in the early hours of this morning. It was the PC's job to check surface shelters like this. He discovered the body and was about to perform first aid, thinking the poor girl might have fainted or something, when he saw what had happened to her. Naturally when he saw that he skedaddled straight off to the nearest police call box and alerted the nearest station. They called us at the Yard and we were here within thirty minutes before the early morning workers came on the scene.'

Major Dalby picked up on that 'naturally'. Why should a special constable 'naturally' drop everything and hurry off to the nearest call box? What was so strange about the dead woman to occasion him to do that? But he decided not to query the point; it was better that the big middle-aged policeman should do things in his own way.

'We've identified her, of course. She's not a local. She's a member of an ATS transport company which had to bring up a convoy of fifteen-hundredweights to the Duke of York's Barracks. Her CO allowed the drivers to stay overnight in the Smoke to see the sights. Most of 'em were from the North. Yorkshire and godforsaken places like that.' Like most Londoners, the Super thought that anything north of Watford was 'abroad'. 'She did – and look what it did for her.'

'What?' Dalby asked quietly, wondering where all this was leading for his own little specialist team. 'Murder?'

'Not just murder, Major,' the policeman said gravely. 'I've seen some things in my time.' He shook his head. 'But nothing . . .' He didn't finish his sentence. Instead he turned to the doctor. 'Can I show the gentlemen the . . .' Again he didn't complete his words.

'Yes. But it's not pleasant.'

'I know that, sir.'

'All right, be it on your own head,' the doctor answered and, taking a deep breath, he pulled back the sheet that covered the lower half of the dead ATS's body.

Mackenzie could not control his shocked gasp. Beneath the tunic she was naked, her khaki knickers and torn woollen stockings rolled down to her ankles, her legs spread wide. Naturally the young Intelligence NCO had seen women in that position before: quite a few to be exact; for the handsome staff sergeant had quite a reputation with the ladies. But never had he seen anything like this: an abomination, a bloody perversion, a desecration of the female body.

The doctor heard the gasp and said softly, 'I warned you. She has been raped and then mutilated. There has been some attempt to remove certain female organs. As you can also see, the breasts –' he lifted the tunic to reveal the dead girl's small breasts – 'have been bitten, around the nipples, quite severely. One has been almost severed.' He pulled the tunic down sharply, as if he couldn't stand the sight himself for any longer.

Dalby licked his suddenly dried-up lips. 'What kind of perverted swine . . . ?' He stopped and continued with, 'How was it done? I mean to her vagina.'

The doctor held up his bloodstained right glove. In it he clasped a jackknife. 'With this. It's one of those army ones, issued to all troops, with all sorts of gadgets a soldier might need in the field. This one has a corkscrew and a tin-opener. That's how it was done.'

Mackenzie felt the hot vomit well up in his throat. But he controlled himself just in time. 'British,' he said thickly to no one in particular.

'Yes, British Army issue,' the Super agreed.

Dalby said, 'Please cover her up, Doctor.'

With a grunt the latter did so, saying, 'I've seen this sort of thing before, a long time ago when I was a young student in Germany. Once the killer gets to this stage, he'll do it again.'

'How do you mean, Doctor?' Dalby asked.

'Rape is relatively common and the rapist gets more than sexual pleasure from taking a woman by force, and if he can get away with it, he'll do it again. But some beast who does this kind of thing is going beyond rape, he's after sexual satisfaction, and he's after power – sexual power – but on a whole new level.'

Trying to keep his voice steady, Mackenzie said, 'I understand that, Doctor, but why do you say that a monster of this kind will do it again? What's the justification?'

The doctor sniffed, as if he felt he was wasting his time with a fool. 'Don't you see? Sex, especially now in wartime with all the loose girls and whores, can be easily obtained. War always does that to the human race – they want to – er – fuck all the time. So our monster can find a woman easily enough – for sex. And once he's got a willing woman to the stage that she's prepared for sex, he wants to go a step further. He wants to mutilate her. That would be for him the ultimate thrill, even better than copulation. Don't ask me the full psychology of the matter because I don't understand it myself. But I'm prepared to lay odds on this. If he gets away with this one, he'll do it again.' With that he pulled off his bloodstained gloves and with an air of finality snapped the clasp of his old-fashioned Gladstone bag closed.

Outside they waited till the doctor pedalled away on his squeaky old bike and the ambulance had taken the body of the poor young mutilated ATS girl inside, her blood dripping through the canvas of the stretcher as the two men had done so. Then the Super lit yet another Player and said, 'There's a coffee stall further down the road and with a bit o' luck I can get us a bacon sandwich, if you like, gentlemen. Black market, of course.' He shrugged. 'But so what.'

Mackenzie knew what he meant. In the light of what they had just experienced what did a black-market bacon sandwich amount to? But both he and Dalby declined the offer. Neither of them felt in the mood for the delights of an illegal sandwich. Both their minds were still full of the sight of those bloody mutilated loins.

The Super must have been able to read their minds, for he said, 'I can understand you ain't got much appetite this morning. Must have been the same all those years ago when they first discovered Jack the Ripper's first victim, not more than five minutes away from here.' He laughed without conviction when he saw the look on the two Army men's faces. 'Yes, this is Jack the Ripper country, you know . . . five minutes away from here.'

'Good grief!' Mackenzie exclaimed. But his boss, Dalby, remained silent.

The Super pulled himself up, as if he had abruptly realized what he had just said and the conclusions that an imaginative person might draw from his words. 'Never mind the sawbones. Old Doc Pearson, he's our police surgeon, has always been a bit of a nervous nelly. We never let him get us into a tizzy. So I don't think you ought to pay much heed to what he says about a repeat of what happened in the air-raid shelter.'

Dalby nodded. Still he didn't say anything. But his mind was racing. He hadn't liked what he had seen this day – first the suicide of the German spy and then the poor slaughtered body of the young female soldier. But neither of these things were relevant to the greater scheme of things as far as his Special Intelligence unit was concerned. His voice revealing nothing, he said, wondering if now he might find out why they had been summoned to this sordid case on 'highest authority', 'Superintendent, I've been told that you were to keep anything found here relating to the military for me.'

'Oh yes, I nearly forgot.' The policeman reached inside his heavy dark overcoat. 'There's not much. Here's the poor girl's pay book, with a few personal photos inside.' He handed over the brown-covered document. 'Her pass for twenty-four hours' leave. And then this. We found it under her body, the poor dear. Looks like one of those new-fangled unit titles to me – Parachute Regiment, Reconnaissance Corps – that the lads wear on the shoulders of their battledress. Perhaps it belonged to one of her boyfriends or something.'

Dalby stared at the cloth strip with its green embroidered title. '*R . . . A . . . N . . . G . . . E . . . R!*' he spelled it out aloud. 'Ranger.' It didn't mean anything to him.

# Two

The Prime Minister was obviously afflicted by one of his moods of despair, what he himself called 'the black dog'. It was a periodic thing with Winston Churchill and Dalby, who had briefed the PM before, guessed it stemmed from the great responsibilities that this sixty-five-year-old man bore on his fat shoulders. After all, since Dunkirk, Churchill had virtually single-handedly kept Britain in the war through the time when the country had fought Germany alone, suffering defeat after defeat.

Dalby, the veteran of the trenches of World War One, when men's lives were thrown away so recklessly by the 'frocks', as the frontline soldiers had called the London politicians contemptuously, was no great friend of the 'Whitehall Warriors'. But his heart went out to the old man, as he slumped there, head in hands, opposite him, not even touching his midday glass of brandy. All the same he couldn't understand why the PM was so affected by the fact that a Ranger shoulder patch had been found near the body of the murdered girl. Soldiers killed girls in moments of passion quite often in wartime; it was something they were trained to do – kill. And brutalized as these young men sometimes were by the strains of combat, it was something to be expected of them when their strained nerves snapped. Why should the fact that one of these new boys, the Yanks, had committed a similar crime, as horrific as it was, affect the PM in this matter?

It was as if Churchill could read Dalby's thoughts. For abruptly he raised his head from his arms and growled in that familiar tone of his that sent the shivers down the spine of everyone who had listened to his pronouncements over the BBC these last years, 'Nothing, but nothing, must injure the reputation of the soldiers that President Roosevelt has sent over here in his great generosity, while they are in the UK.' He looked challengingly at Dalby, thrusting out that pugnacious jaw of his as if he half expected the soldier to give him an argument.

But nothing was further from Dalby's mind. He kept his peace. Churchill was too dangerous an opponent.

'I have spent a great deal of time since 1940, Major, trying to convince the President to enter this great crusade against Nazism. Finally in December, he and his great country joined us in the struggle against infamy. In the course of time more and more American soldiers will arrive here until we are finally in a position to take the war from this island across the Channel and into the heart of the enemy's homeland.'

Normally Dalby, a dry rational man, would not have been impressed by the old-fashioned rhetoric the old man used. Not now, however. He knew it was Churchill's determination and use of words which had brought Britain through crisis after crisis. From Churchill he accepted the nineteenth-century style of oratory without criticism.

'But that will take time, Major. Till then we must ensure that the reputation of the American soldier in this country remains unsullied. The Americans speak our language and I, personally, often refer to them as our cousins from across the sea. In reality they are not. They are often brash, naive and, in many ways, totally different from us. That, our

49

people will find out. More importantly there are many in this country in leading positions who actively dislike the Americans.' Churchill wagged a stubby finger under Dalby's nose, as if in warning. 'We must not let that sort of person dictate what the ordinary Englishman thinks of the American. Is that clear, Major?'

'Yessir!' Dalby answered promptly, wondering what all this high-level stuff had to do with Intelligence and the murder and mutilation of a poor innocent ATS girl in a surburban air-raid shelter.

Churchill enlightened him immediately, while outside in the corridor, one of the commissionaires was singing softly to himself. *'And this is number one and I've got her on the run . . . roll me over and do it again . . . roll me over in the clover . . .'*

Dalby frowned and then next instant wondered at the incongruity of the situation: here, Churchill, concerned, seemingly, with the larger politics of the global conflict; out there a humble ex-serviceman singing the latest ribald soldier's marching song. Churchill, for his part, did not appear to hear the commissionaire, who was now launching into verse number two, *'And this is number two and I've got it up her flue . . . roll me over and do it again . . .'* He was saying, 'It is for this reason I have called you, our top man in Special Intelligence, to deal with this matter. I did so immediately I heard of the murder of that poor girl and the possibility that she might have been murdered by an American serviceman. You know what the press would do with a story like that, especially rags like the *Daily Mirror.'*

Dalby didn't know what the press would do with such a story. Nor was he interested. His attention had been grabbed at once by Churchill's statement about the murder being committed possibly by an American serviceman.

He dared to interrupt Churchill's monologue with, 'You say an American serviceman, sir. Can I ask why, Prime Minister?'

'You can. Because there are only a handful of Americans in this country at this time. Most of the US V Corps is in Northern Ireland, as you perhaps know, but there is one major US unit training in England at the moment. It is a new unit set up on the lines of our British Commando. Colonel Lucian Truscott, its commander, is outside to brief you further on these "Rangers" of theirs.'

Dalby got it. The patch found near the dead girl's body had borne the title 'Ranger'. Was that the connection? He didn't hesitate. 'You mean, sir, that the murderer might have been one of these Rangers currently in the UK?'

'Yes, Major.'

'I see.'

'I hope you do, Major Dalby. Because if this is the case and it comes out, you can imagine the outcry from certain sections of the press. First Yank unit involved in murder of innocent English girl . . . sort of thing.'

'But we can't hush up the matter altogether, sir, even with censorship, if one of these Rangers did kill the ATS girl,' Dalby protested, attempting indirectly to get away from a sordid murder investigation and get on with what he regarded as his main job – fighting the Hun and his evil machinations in the world of espionage – the war in the shadows.

Churchill looked at him evenly. 'Can't we, Major?' he said simply.

'But—' Dalby began, but Churchill waved him to silence with a curt movement of his pudgy hand.

'There are ways and means, Major. Now let us concentrate on the problem at hand. I suggest you talk to Colonel Truscott of the Rangers.' He bent over his desk once more, spectacles apparently just about to fall off the end of his stubby nose. The unknown commissionaire was disappearing down the corridor singing the bawdy song still: '*Now this is number three and he's got her against a tree . . . Roll me over in the clover and do it again . . .*' Major Dalby stood there for a moment longer, puzzled and confused about what to do next until he realized that in the manner of all great men, for whom every minute was precious, he was being dismissed. Awkwardly he saluted. Churchill didn't look up. His mind was already on other things . . .

'It's like this, Major,' Truscott explained easily, sitting swinging his booted leg to and fro as he lectured the stony-faced Britisher, whom he'd heard was a big shot in limey intelligence. 'My boss in the States, General Marshall, Chief-of-Staff to the US Army, is keen on a cross-Channel invasion this year. But he's a smart old bird. He knows that the Army is willing, but that there's no substitute for battle experience. If your trained Commandos are going to lead that invasion, as they will, and we Yanks are going to go into action with them, we need to learn from the experts.' He gave Dalby a gold-toothed smile, but Dalby didn't respond. His mind was busy with other matters.

'So Marshall decided America had to form an outfit just like the Commandos, to be trained with them and gain from their two-year experience in combat. As we couldn't use the name Commando, we decided on a good old-fashioned Yankee name – the Rangers. They were formed back in the eighteenth century to fight against the Indians and the French—'

'I know.' Dalby decided to interrupt the American, who was likeable but long-winded. 'We formed them, you know. There are still units in the British Army who date back to that time in North America. The Rifle Brigade, the South Lancs Regiment and the like.'

For a moment Truscott was caught off guard. Then he laughed and said, 'OK, Major, forgive me for bullshitting you.'

Now it was Dalby's turn to give one of his rare smiles.

''Kay, so we asked for volunteers from the two US divisions here in the UK. We got two thousand. Of them we picked just over five hundred. We selected them on the basis of a rigorous physical examination. They had to have twenty-twenty vision, no eyeglasses, no movable dentures, no night blindness. We gave them in-depth interviews on their mental outlook.' He grinned. 'We didn't interview 'em naked like your Commando volunteers, to stress them while they were buck-assed nude. That would be going too far. But we did satisfy ourselves that they were top-class both physically *and* mentally.'

Dalby absorbed the American colonel's information before asking, 'You've had no problems with them, Colonel? You know – absent without leave, even desertion, getting into trouble with the local women – that sort of thing.'

Truscott's grin broadened. 'Hell, your Commando boys work 'em too hard for them to get up to tricks. They're exhausted at night, I know I was when I went through that Commando assault course. I sure was dragging my ass after that – and I thought I was top-fit. Women?' He shrugged. 'I guess they would if they could. After all they are young guys, full o' piss and vinegar. The best age.' He shrugged. 'But if you'll forgive my French, Major. The only thing that's available at that Commando training centre of yours is sheep. And I don't think my boys are that desperate just now that they'd try to gain a little carnal knowledge of our four-legged woolly friends.'

Dalby shared his smile. 'Take your point, Colonel.' He was serious again. 'But how do you explain the fact that there was a Ranger shoulder title found at the scene of the girl's murder? It's a pretty rare shoulder title. Indeed, I didn't know the Rangers existed till this morning myself. How do you explain its presence in that air-raid shelter in London, a good hundred-odd miles from the Commando training camp, sir?'

Truscott's smile vanished. 'Quite frankly,' he answered, 'I can't. It's a damned mystery. You know that this whole Ranger project is supposed to be "most secret", as you English call it. Nobody in general is to know we're in England at the moment. As far as the British public is concerned, the US Army in Europe, in the shape of the US V Corps, is in Ireland. You see, Major, we've got our first combat mission planned and we want to keep everything very hush-hush.'

'May I ask where?' Dalby ventured. The more he knew about these mysterious Rangers the better, for he had a sneaking feeling that he was going to have a lot to do with them before he was finished.

Truscott hesitated, then he said, sweeping his arm around at their surroundings, 'I guess, dealing with Mr Churchill and all this, you'll have the top security clearance.'

Dalby nodded that he had.

'Well.' Truscott lowered his voice. 'We're going into North Africa, French North Africa. It's an operation cooked up by the Joint Chiefs of Staff at the orders of FDR –' he meant the American President, Franklin Delano Roosevelt – 'and your Mr Churchill. We think the French there will be receptive to our invasion and in due course, after minimal resistance, we can join up with your Eighth Army coming up from Egypt.'

'Excellent!' Dalby exclaimed with feigned enthusiasm.

The British 8th Army had been in the Western Desert for two years now and they still hadn't achieved a victory there. Indeed at the moment it didn't look as if they would ever gain the upper hand, especially against the Hun, the so-called 'Desert Fox', Marshal Rommel. But he wasn't going to tell the 'new boy' Truscott that; he still believed, in his American innocence, that once you believed you'd win, you would. It seemed as simple as that for the Yanks.

'So you can see, Major, we don't want any publicity for our Rangers.'

'Agreed. But there is still the business of this nasty murder. That's got to be cleared up.'

'You'll get every assistance we can give you, Major,' Truscott said slowly and thoughtfully, rubbing his big square jaw as if something was troubling him suddenly.

Outside, the sirens were beginning their mournful wail, heralding another of the new German 'hit-and-run raids'. These attacks were nothing like the raids by hundreds of German planes in the winter of 1940–41. Still, they kept the population on their toes, making them nervous and eager to get under cover to the smelly, abandoned shelters – just in case. At this moment, Dalby reasoned there'd be hundreds, thousands, of frightened women running through the streets of London trying to find a shelter from the bombs that might well soon come raining down. An ideal situation for a murderer like the unknown who had killed the ATS girl, who might be looking to make a new conquest who might well end up dead and mutilated as she had done. The thought lent urgency to his question. 'Colonel, I hope you don't mind my asking this – I realize you are very proud of your men and your new command.'

Truscott, who had been looking at the sky a little nervously, for this would be his first experience of an enemy bombing raid, turned his attention back to Dalby. 'Yes, I am proud of my Rangers. Please ask your question, Major.'

'Well, sir, it's this. Are any of your Rangers unaccounted for?'

'How do you mean?'

'I mean, undertaking the kind of Commando training your Rangers are currently doing, there are bound to be some of them injured and perhaps in hospital. But apart from those people, who I am sure are accounted for, do you have any other Rangers who are on leave, say, or perhaps –' Dalby risked the question, though he guessed that Truscott would be touchy about such matters – 'absent without leave – even deserters?'

Dalby had guessed right. Truscott suddenly looked very stern. 'Remember, Major, my Rangers are all volunteers. Out of two thousand GIs who volunteered to leave a relatively easy existence in Northern Ireland, we accepted only five hundred-odd, who didn't know what they were letting themselves in for when we accepted them. Now –' he leaned forward and tapped Dalby on the knee as if he wished to emphasize the point – 'do you think such men would desert, even if they could get out of the Commando camp, which is guarded and sealed off by your own troops, by the way?'

Reluctantly Dalby had to agree that the US colonel was right.

'So, for your information, Major, we have only one Ranger at this moment who is not in the camp. He was injured in an incident involving one of your Commando officers who was either overzealous or hated Americans . . .' Swiftly Truscott sketched in the story of O'Corrigan and the grenade-throwing incident, while Dalby half-listened, already aware of the thud-thud of the capital's anti-aircraft guns to the east and the steady drone of the German bombers getting ever closer.

'And what happened to this Lieutenant O'Corrigan, sir?' Dalby asked without too much interest when Truscott was finished with his story.

'The tough bastard beat it, Major. Knocked out a couple of military-police cops and high-tailed it from the camp. Somehow or other he managed to get hold of a vehicle. It was found abandoned where it had run out of gas – excuse me, petrol to you English – and that was the last we've seen of Mr O'Corrigan up to the present.'

Dalby bit his bottom lip thoughtfully, the impending attack forgotten for a moment. 'Was he a good officer, this Englishman?'

'Irish – bog Irishman,' Truscott corrected him hastily. The bombers were almost on top of them now. Outside in the street, the wardens were shrilling their whistles in warning and the duty policemen were putting on their steel helmets and crying urgently, *'Take shelter now . . . please take cover!'*

'Excellent. Tremendous war record. Your Military Cross in France in '40. A Bar to it in Crete in '41. They said he wiped out a squad of Kraut paratroopers single-handed in the first days of the German paradrop there. Recommended for the Distinguished Service Order in Egypt. Didnt get it, however.'

'Why?'

'Because of his temper. He socked his commanding officer in the jaw when his CO tried to break off a hopeless action with the enemy.' Truscott forced a grin and wished the hard-faced Intelligence man would let him off the hook now and allow them to run to the shelters. 'Not a wise thing for a junior captain to do. He was demoted and didn't get the medal. A few days later he was apparently badly wounded and sent back to Great Britain to recover. He volunteered for the Commando as soon as he could walk. Although he wasn't really fit enough for the Commando, they took him – with his record.'

'A violent man then?'

'*Very*. Typically Irish. A nice enough guy normally. A real charmer, they say, with the women. But when he gets his paddy up –' Truscott forced a rather dry whistle – 'watch out for the thunder and lightning.'

'Hm,' Dalby mused. 'Might be a person we could look into.'

'Sure. But you've got to find him first, Major, and the O'Corrigans of this world are hard guys to find. You—' The piercing whistle of the first bomb hurtling down cut into the rest of his words. In an instant Colonel Truscott was on his feet, yelling above that sinister howl, 'Come on, Major, let's beat it before those Krauts do for us.'

Obediently Major Dalby followed his advice and 'beat it'. But even as he headed for the Downing Street shelter, hurried on by the urgent cries of the policeman sheltering in the doorway of nearby Number Eleven, he told himself that Staff Sergeant Mackenzie's first task on the morrow would be to look more closely into the record of that particular 'bog Irishman', O'Corrigan.

# Three

'*Platoon, platoon* – eyes right!'
The skinny little second lieutenant's voice was almost drowned by the clatter of a shunting engine over at Paddington Station. He looked a little worried. Had the marching soldiers heard him? They had. Laden down with full Field Service Marching Order, weapons and steel helmets, they responded well enough. As the boy raised his brown-gloved hand to salute the senior officer seeing off the draft for North Africa, their eyes clicked as one to the right. All save one.

He was a tall lean soldier, who looked older than the rest. He stumbled as if he had suddenly been attacked by nausea and the like. The platoon sergeant bringing up the rear of the draft hissed out of the side of his mouth, 'All right, laddie, fall out and make yer own bleeding way to the train before yon colonel sees yer. And mind you get there – I've my eagle eye on yer.'

'Ta, sarge,' the tall soldier said, also out of the side of his mouth. 'Just get mesen a drink o' water from them WVS ladies and I'll be right as rain. Ta, agen.' He dropped back as the rest of the platoon clattered on to the platform and the waiting train which would take them to their own particular date with destiny.

Abruptly recovered, the tall man, carrying his heavy load of equipment effortlessly, pushed his way in the general direction of the WVS stall, where good ladies wearing large hats, looking like female cowboys in tweed, were serving tea in jam jars to crowds of waiting soldiers. *You soldiers can't have cups – you always break them unnecessarily.* His hard blue eyes were everywhere as he surveyed the crowded scene of the typical wartime station, alert for the least sign of danger.

There seemed to be none. Everyone, sad or happy, appeared to be totally concerned with his own affairs. There were lordly officers, sniggering a lot and talking in too loud voices; humble shabby privates, laden down like pack mules with kit, just like the tall man; red-eyed womenfolk and squalling kids; pale-faced military clerks with different coloured bands around their sleeves to indicate their function; hard-eyed military policemen, armed with revolvers, granite-faced and suspicious – and in the shadows the ever-present whores, thrusting out their stomachs suggestively and whispering in gruff voices, 'Fancy a bit, ducky? Give yer a fly wank for five bob . . .'

But the tall man wasn't looking for that kind of cheap tart. He had another woman in mind. But first he had to get off the station. He had no pass. What documents he possessed in the pocket of his battledress blouse, his pay book and the like, described a man half his size, who wore glasses, which he didn't; and the man to whom those documents belonged was presumably telling his sad story to the Regimental Police at Bovington Camp.

He thrust his way through a group of bandy-legged little jocks, drinking the sugarless tea, and by the looks of their beetroot-coloured faces, it wasn't only tea they had been drinking on their long journey from the north. Indeed, he could smell the pungent odour of whisky even above the smell of smoke and cinders given off by the locomotives lined up at the various platforms.

The big man paused and shifted his load, as if the big pack was too much for him. Out of the corner of his eyes, he saw that the MPs guarding the barrier had been changed. The new lot he knew from experience would be keen for a while, at least half an hour or so into their shift, before they'd relax and check only the documents of any serviceman who appeared suspicious to them. But he knew, too, he couldn't wait half an hour. The draft would have gone by then. And he would stick out like a sore thumb, laden down with FSO Marching Order and wearing the black beret of the Royal Tank Regiment as they were.

'What frigging kinda char is this?' the drunken Gordon Highlander next to him complained peering down at the dark brown liquid in his jam jar. 'Nae milk, nae sugar – and plenty o' yon bromide I bet too, so a feller cannae get a hard on.' He cast a dark look at the good lady of the WVS in her green tweed suit, who was nearest him on the crowded platform.

'Now none of that kind of talk, young man,' the WVS chided him briskly in the manner of a woman who was used to the childish behaviour of young soldiers. 'Remember where you are.'

'I ken where I'm staying,' the drunk Jock answered bitterly. 'I'm on my way to get ma bluidy fool head blown off fer yer high-falutin' bluidy Sassenachs.'

'I've warned you,' she said severely, hitching up her substantial bosom, which had appeared to sag. 'Any more of that kind of talk, and *I'll* call the redcaps.'

'Stuff yer frigging redcaps!' the Jock said and in that same instant dropped his jam jar on the platform, crying defiantly, 'And that's what ye can do with yer frigging tea, as well.'

The dropped jam jar seemed to be the signal for the rest of his drunken comrades to do the same, while a young officer cried, 'Stand fast, the Gordons! Do you hear, stand fast!'

But the 1st Battalion the Gordon Highlanders, famed as they were on the battlefield for standing fast in the face of the charging enemy, were not prepared to do so on this late spring day on Paddington Station; even though the hated redcaps at the ticket barrier were shrilling their whistles and preparing to attack.

The tall lean soldier saw his chance. He threw off his great pack. 'Fuck this for a game o' sodjers, mates,' he cried. 'Don't let the red-capped bastards get yer down.' He dived forward and slammed into the WVS woman. Caught totally off guard, she went down, legs spread and high in the air to reveal her pink bloomers reaching down to below her fat knees. 'Up the Gordons!' someone yelled. 'Scotland fer ever!' another cried. Then in an instant all was chaos and mass confusion. Whistles shrilled. Irate officers bellowed orders. The RTO drew his pistol and pointed it at the roof. Children screamed and a whore who had dropped her purse with the shock and had bent down to pick it up felt her naked rear being groped by a bespectacled private in the Royal Army Pay Corps – for free! But the tall lean private in the uniform of the Armoured Corps was no longer there to enjoy the spectacle of free enterprise . . .

He turned into the square located between the Edgware Road and Harrow Road. Once the tall Edwardian houses the square contained had been well painted and bright. The brass door knockers had been polished by prim housemaids, their high steps had been immaculately kept by slattern chars, while prim and proper nannies had wheeled their charges down the swept pavements.

But that had been long before. Now the council had taken the houses' railings away as metal scrap for the war effort and the little squares of front gardens were neglected, filled with weeds and the rubbish of the last three years of bombed masonry, abandoned mattresses, cracked sinks and rusty Anderson bomb shelters. A mess.

The tall man in the shabby khaki uniform sighed. He stared up at the buildings, most of their windows criss-crossed with sticky paper against bomb damage. To him, the grimy run-down Edwardian houses seemed to symbolize the England of 1942. It, too, was run-down and shabby, kept going by a sheer effort of will.

Slowly he walked down the empty street, his heavy boots echoing hollowly in that stone chasm. He passed a bomb site. He stared at the fading sign from 1940. It read *Business as usual*. He shrugged. What a weary legend that was. He passed another house, a stovepipe protruding from the lower window. From inside came the sounds of the Andrews Sisters belting out, 'The Boogie-Woogie Bugle Boy of Company B'. With a slight sigh he told himself that the 'New World' had reached even this shabby place.

O'Corrigan sighed again. It seemed to him that people thought the brash Americans with their pushy way of life were the only way ahead for poor old England, or at least the womenfolk appeared to look at it like that. What England was really letting itself in for in the future seemed beyond their comprehension.

He dismissed the English malaise. Instead he concentrated on his own problem. That was more pressing at the moment. So far he had avoided capture and arrest, but then he was an old hand, who knew a lot about the tricks of soldiers who were on the run – 'on the trot', as they called it. Now he was going to try another trick which might give him some respite for a couple of days more. It might give him a chance to find a permanent solution.

*Number Twenty-Two*. That was the address she had given

him in her last letter to the commando camp. Slowly he mounted Twenty-Two's cracked steps. He skirted the pile of dog shit and frowned, as he ran his gaze over the line of nameplates next to the unpolished brass bell pushes – *M'selle Bogex, French lessons and Conversation by Appointment Only*. As worried as he was, the fugitive grinned at that. He could guess what kind of French lessons M'Selle Bogex gave by appointment only . . . *R.G. Roy, BA (Hons) Bombay* . . . *The Great Tidmus, Professional Wrestler* . . . And there it was – *Paula, Exotic Dancer*. She was still at the same address, fans and snake and all. His heart leapt. She was a kindly soul. He felt she'd help him, if anyone would.

Still he had to be careful. The Military Police were no fools. By now they would have been through his correspondence back at the Commando camp, looking for possible contacts he might turn to. He couldn't afford to take chances. He looked at the list again and pressed the button of *The Great Tidmus, Professional Wrestler*.

There was a buzz almost immediately. The door creaked and at the end of the dark passage, which smelled of boiled cabbage and unwashed clothing, a very small man, his hair in paper curlers, peered round his own door and said in a falsetto voice, 'You a promoter?' He giggled and immediately started undoing one of his curlers. 'Oh, I must look a real sight. But you know my public expect it of me,' he simpered.

For once O'Corrigan, the hard man, was confused. He hadn't expected *The Great Tidmus* to be a little nancy boy with his hair in curlers. Hastily, he blurted out, 'I'm sorry. I pressed the wrong button. I wanted – er – Paula.'

The Great Tidmus stopped undoing his curlers at once. His face fell. 'Oh, and I thought you were coming to me – with an offer.' He lowered his head and blinked his eyes a couple of times in what he supposed was a seductive fashion.

'No, Paula, exotic dancer.'

The Great Tidmus puffed out his skinny, lightly rouged cheeks. 'Exotic, my foot . . . and that bloody great snake she keeps up there . . . God only knows what she does with it at night when she goes to bed, but there's one hell of a thumping going on most nights – and the bedsprings squeak,' he added darkly. 'Yer, she's up there all right.' He gave a petulant little shrug of his skinny shoulders, patted the back of his head and disappeared as quickly as he had come.

O'Corrigan shook his head in mock wonder and headed for the rickety stairs. Number Twenty-Two was definitely a funny place, but if all its tenants were like the Great Tidmus, he'd be safe here. No one would suspect an ordinary bloke like himself of anything.

Paula, Exotic Dancer was lying on a rumpled bed as he peered through the door, which was ajar. She was naked save for a shabby torn negligee and from the way she had parted her legs under it it was very clear she wasn't a true blonde. Lying next to her on the bed there was a large snake, which she was tickling in a casual sort of manner, though to O'Corrigan's way of thinking, the reptile needed to be locked up safely right then. But he made no comment. For Paula was exceedingly fond of her snakes, often remarking, 'I'd take a snake any day rather than a man,' which mostly occasioned her to laugh when she remembered what her naked act with the snake was supposed to make most of her male spectators think of. 'Hello, big boy,' she said in that fake American accent of hers (in reality she came from Rochdale) as if it was every day that she received male visitors lying nearly naked on her bed toying with a huge, dangerous-looking snake.

'Come for a little comfort?' She winked knowingly, not realizing that her false eyelashes were hanging at an angle; perhaps the snake had been playing with *her*.

'In a way,' he said hesitantly, pushing the fatigue cap to the back of his head wearily. 'Need a kip for a couple of days or so.'

'Be my guest,' she answered. 'But you'll have to share the bed with the snake as well as me.'

'Thanks. I'll try, Paula. Got a drink?'

'Sure,' she answered and swung herself off the bed – very carelessly. Her ample breasts swinging from side to side, she went to the mantelpiece, heavy with bottles of gin and whisky, probably given to her by her many 'admirers', as she called her clients. For she was getting old, and exotic dancers were not much in demand at a time when there were plenty of amateurs who were prepared to do more than wave feathers about for the price of a gin and lemon.

He had met her back in '40 just after he had returned from Dunkirk, filled with rage and resentment at the way the British Army had been flung out of the Continent after a campaign that had lasted a mere two weeks. She'd been a *Celebrated Lancashire Clog Dancer* then, trained by Gracie Fields personally. That had been a downright lie, but the troops hadn't minded, especially when she did one of her short-skirted twirls and discovered to her dismay and the troops' delight, 'Sorry, lads, I forgot to pull on my knicks – I was so excited at the thought of meeting all you big strong heroes.'

Thereupon she had given them another twirl and stamp of her clogs. Next to him the Padre had blushed and he'd muttered something about 'disgraceful', but a grinning O'Corrigan had noted he'd peered very hard through his tortoiseshell glasses all the same. He'd taken her over to the mess that night and although she was wise to the ways of soldiers, she'd downed a couple of stiff gins before announcing, 'All right, luv, you deserve it after Dunkirk. Come on, get me to your room, General, and I'll see if I can make yer eyes pop.' And she had, too.

He'd seen her a couple of times after his return from North Africa and she'd been very proud of him and his Military Cross. Indeed she had become very ladylike and 'cut-glass', as she put it, now that he was an officer and gent. With a medal for bravery with it, to boot. Now, however, she said, as she brought him his drink, 'You're in trouble, ain't yer?' The accent was pure Rochdale once more. 'Otherwise why are yer dressed as a private and without yer medal?'

He took a stiff drink from the whisky she had poured him, without adding water, as if she had already realized that he needed it. He knew it was no use lying to Paula. She might have left her elementary school at the age of fourteen with not much in the way of an education. But she was wise to the ways of the world and, in particular, those of men. So he said quite openly, 'I've deserted. I'm on the run from the redcaps. I need somewhere to bed down till I can figure out what to do next.'

Paula's attitude changed at once. 'Freddie, get off the bleeding bed,' she snapped at the big snake. 'Me and the gentleman here have got something to discuss. Go on – bugger off!' To emphasize her words, she gave the snake a hefty slap. For a moment it bared its fangs and O'Corrigan, as brave as he was, felt an icy finger of fear trace its way down his spine. But the snake did as it was ordered. With an eerie slithering sound, it uncoiled itself and slid under the rumpled bed, knocking the chamberpot as it did so.

'You poor dear,' Paula said soothingly, as if she was still talking to Freddie. 'After all you've done and suffered for your country. Fancy doing that to you.' She reached out to his head and pressed it between her great breasts, so that the Irishman felt he might be suffocated if she didn't let go soon. She did and when she spoke again, her tone was very reasonable, but still concerned.

'I know you, you big Mick. You and your hot temper. You've gorn and punched yer CO agen, ain't yer?'

He shook his head sadly. 'No, worse than that this time, dear old Paula.'

'How worse?'

'I've killed an American – accidentally of course. But they won't believe me. An American Ranger. They're up in arms about it . . .' He let his voice trail away to nothing, as if he were realizing for the first time just how serious his situation was.

'*Crikey!*' Her plump be-ringed hand flew to her mouth in alarm. 'A Yank? Cor, ferk a duck. They ain't been over here no time. I ain't even had one as a customer yet—' She stopped abruptly, as if she had suddenly thought of something. 'Ranger did you say, Rory?'

'That's right. They're a kind of American commando. Or they will be. Hey, what do you know about the Rangers, Paula?'

But she wasn't listening. She was fumbling with a newspaper that lay at the bottom of the bed, shaking out the bits and pieces of offal upon which she fed the snake. 'Here,' she said, handing him the bloodstained *News of the World*. 'Take a gander at that. I get it every Sunday with *War Cry* down at the pub. I like to read the dirty bits.'

'What?' he asked, puzzled.

'That picture next to the "*Vicar Accused*" bit.'

O'Corrigan then saw the illustration. It was in black and white and not in the green of the badge he had come to know. But he recognized it immediately. It was that of the Rangers. Below it, there was a short piece which told him nothing really. It read simply: *Eyewitnesses sought: persons seeing this badge worn by person(s) in uniform recently in London. Please contact New Scotland Yard, or your local police station.*

It was a perfectly innocuous piece of the kind readers encountered in newspapers every day in wartime, when the authorities didn't want to give away such information over the airways through the BBC. But O'Corrigan, his heart racing suddenly, was aware of Paula staring at him hard as he read the piece aloud. 'So?' he asked, laying the paper on the bed.

'So,' she echoed, face firm and almost angry-looking. 'You worked with these here Rangers, killed one of them. Accidentally. And now yer on the trot.'

'Go on,' he urged. 'Let's have it out,' he said, wondering where she was going with all this.

'Well, Rory, let's face it. The rozzers wouldn't put that in the papers just because you've committed a military crime or even just because you've deserted, would they?'

He nodded his agreement, but said nothing. He knew she had something else up her sleeve and he was waiting for her to let him have it.

'On Friday they said on the Forces Programme that there'd been an ATS killed here in London. They said, too, that the rozzers were looking for a soldier in connection with that murder.' She paused and looked quizzically at the red-haired Irishman before saying, 'Is that the link between you and the Ranger armband?' She licked her lips, as if they were suddenly very dry.

'God Almighty, Paula,' O'Corrigan exploded. 'You don't think I'd kill anybody?'

'Yes, I do,' she answered stoutly. 'You've already killed somebody. You told me yer have yersen.' She looked hard at him. 'You killed Jerries to win that gong of yours.'

'I know . . . I know,' he protested. 'But they were men, Paula, armed men – the enemy. This is a woman, if you've told it right. Look at me, Paula, do you think I'd ever kill a woman?'

She nodded her head with a certain degree of reluctance. 'All right . . . all right, luv. Thousands wouldn't but I do. I believe yer. It wasn't you who saw off the woman. But I bet my bottom dollar that this Ranger is involved in the murder. And you was with the Rangers and now yer on the trot. You're the most likely suspect.'

'I know,' Rory O'Corrigan said miserably. 'But I'm gonna clear my name some way or other if it's the last thing I do.'

She nodded her understanding and said, 'All the same, Rory O'Corrigan, you'd better get it through yer thick Mick skull that the rozzers all over the Smoke will be out looking for you.' She sniffed and pushed the snake's head back beneath the bed. Again it banged into her tin chamberpot. 'Rory, at this moment, yer right up the creek without a bloody paddle . . .'

# Book Two: Lady Daisy Takes a Hand

'Travelling singly in Piccadilly was virtually
suicide for an unwary GI.'
*William A. Bostick, 1943*

# One

The ancient waiters in their rusty tailcoats creaked back and forth bearing discreetly covered silver dishes. Even the best of restaurants had to be discreet in these black-market days; hence the covers. For, beneath, there were thick red chateaubriand steaks and braces of succulent partridges in red wine sauce. Officially the menu was priced at the government top level of seven shillings and sixpence, but here the patrons were prepared to pay four times more than that for a meal which didn't consist of scrambled dry eggs, whale steak, or a plat du jour which turned out to be minced meat rissoles.

Here most of the diners were civilian. Rich elderly ladies with purple permanent waves and rapacious hungry eyes, not only for the food either. The men were obviously 'important'. They had hard calculating eyes and mouths like rat traps. More often than not they whispered a lot as if what they had to say was not meant for the ears of the waiters and suchlike common folk.

There were a few officers in uniform. But they, too, were middle-aged and 'important', their immaculate service dress, all polished Sam Browne and glittering insignia of rank, adorned with the red tabs of the staff. Usually they were in the company of a girl, very pretty and attentive, and more often than not half their age.

Colonel Tidmuss-Smythe was no different than the rest

73

save that he was older and looked it too with his discreetly dyed hair. But he did wear the dull-red ribbon of the Victoria Cross on his chest among the many other campaign ribbons dating back to the turn of the century. His companion, Daisy, Lady Gore-Allways, was just as pretty and admiring as the rest of the young women present there this day, save that she wore the uniform of a Wren, the Royal Naval female auxiliary. 'I simply couldn't accept a commission, darling. After all, that's what this war is about, the *people*! Besides, khaki makes me look dreadful.' Still, she was no fool and this lunchtime she was going to twist her boss around her finger; and she knew the best way to do it with the old goat. *Sex!*

The colonel clicked his fingers at one of the elderly waiters. He shuffled across with the reckless abandon of a Home Guard with a bad case of the rheumatics. 'Colonel?' he enquired. At the restaurant everyone knew the colonel; he was very generous with tips.

'Another bottle of bubbly, George,' the colonel said. 'And make it toot-sweet, as the Frogs say. Haw, haw!' He guffawed at what he thought was his wit.

'Right away, sir.' The waiter shuffled away and the colonel, his horse teeth giving her one of his lecherous grins, slid his hand under the table again and let his greedy gnarled fingers crawl up Daisy's black-stockinged leg.

She giggled. 'Have you had enough of them yet, sir?' she queried, meaning the non-regulation black silk stockings.

'Can't get enough of them, my dear,' he chortled. 'You know the old joke about the lady of the night who always wore black stockings in memory of all the chaps who had gone over the top – of her stockings, of course. Ha, ha!'

Daisy giggled as she was expected to do by the dirty old bugger who probably hadn't gone over the top these many years, as he fumbled in an attempt to undo her suspender clip. For what reason she didn't know. Surely he wasn't going to try his luck here in the crowded black-market restaurant.

Just at that moment the old waiter came back with the bottle of ice-cold champagne. Reluctantly the old goat withdrew his hand from between her spread legs and waited till the waiter had poured the French champagne at ten pound a bottle.

He touched her glass with his. 'Bottoms up, old dear,' he toasted her.

'What a quaint expression,' she tempted him, knowing already what he would say. 'Where do you hear such expressions?'

'My chaps. Rough working-class types. Salt of the earth though. Mind you –' he winked – 'I wouldn't want them to see your crisp little bottom, you delightful wench you. And don't call me colonel.' He drained his glass greedily. 'Call me Randolph, Randy for short. Or Charley!'

'All right – er – Randy. But of course, outside here I'll have to call you colonel and salute you.'

Once again he he-hawed like some old mule braying. 'I prefer you to salute me in bed, Daisy, what?'

She lowered her eyes as if embarrassed, which she wasn't in the slightest.

'Oh Randy, you are a devil!'

'Always have been – with the ladies. Hello –' he forgot the prospect of bed for a moment – 'there's the one-o'clock news.'

Important as they were, concerned with their own lives, even these people were addicted to the news bulletins, as were the general populace of the embattled island; for they all realized that their own fates were bound up with the course of the war. There was no escaping Britain. If things went wrong, rich and poor alike, they would all suffer.

There was the usual stuff about the usual defeats and 'strategic withdrawals' in the Western Desert, followed by the usual optimistic details of the damage the RAF had caused in last night's raids on the Reich, all carefully balanced to counteract the mess the 8th Army seemed to be making of the only real front for the British Army. Then there were a couple of items in sport. The nation, it seemed, couldn't live without its football matches. Here the announcer's upper-class cheery voice fell a key as he stated, 'There has been another murder in the East End of London. A servicewoman has been found strangled to death. Previously to that she had been sexually interfered with . . .'

'I say, old girl,' the colonel said, as the announcer ceased speaking to be replaced by Joe Loss and his band playing, *Don't sit under the apple tree with anyone else but me . . . but me . . .* 'Got to be damned careful. That's the second young woman in uniform to be murdered in the last week. People are talking about another Ripper. Apparently the first young woman had some pretty awful things done to her – er – undercarriage.' He coughed as if he were suddenly embarrassed and wanted to hide it.

'Don't worry about me, Colonel,' she answered. 'I'm a big girl. I can look after myself. You have to learn to do so in the Wrens.'

He admired her bosom, which was sticking through her brilliant white shirt in its full splendour and said, 'I can see you're a big girl, Daisy. But you know how strong men are when they want – er – their wicked way with a damsel.'

*I do*, she told herself, *but not with you, old boy*. Aloud she said, 'I'm flattered you're so concerned about me, Colonel.'

'Don't call me Colonel, Daisy. It's so damned formal. Call me Randy like the chaps in the mess do.' His hand went a little further up her skirt. She even thought she could hear the old goat beginning to pant a little. A sudden vision of 'Randy' on top of her, naked, pumping away with his wrinkled arse and spindly legs, flashed through her mind. It was horrible. Deftly she caught his wrist and thrust his hand back down her silk-clad thighs, saying, 'Now Randy, you're getting me all wet and passionate.'

'I say, am I?' he said as if amazed himself at her reaction. 'That's good, isn't it, old girl?'

'It is. But not in a public place like this, Randy. What would you do, if I got all excited and started making funny noises, eh?'

'Yes, I suppose you're right.'

'Of course I am, Randy. Besides, there is a time and place for everything, you know.'

'By Gad, I hope you mean that,' he said enthusiastically and took a hasty drink of his bubbly, as if he were abruptly very thirsty.

She knew that the time had come to take the plunge. At this moment, the old goat would do anything if he thought he was going to bed her at some time in the near future. 'I say, Randy,' she said. 'I wonder if I could have the rest of the day, reporting in at zero-eight-hundred tomorrow morning?'

The colonel frowned. 'Bit tricky, m'dear,' he muttered. 'The War Shop is sending somebody over after lunch. He'll want to see all the combined staff present and correct.'

'If he queries it, Randy darling, tell him that one of your female staff – me – is not feeling well. You know –' she rolled her eyes and pressed his skinny knee – 'that time of the month.'

'I say, old dear,' the colonel exclaimed, 'steady on. Can't talk like that to a staff brigadier, you know. *Time of the month . . .*'

She pressed her fingers deeper into his bony knee. 'I'll make it up to you, Randy,' she whispered seductively.

'By Gad!' The colonel licked his lips. 'I say, that's damned sporting of you, Daisy. All right, let's finish off the champers and then you can be away till tomorrow morning. But I'll hold you to your promise, Daisy, you naughty girl.'

'Don't be afraid, I'll keep it, Randy,' she lied glibly, knowing that the skinny old twat had probably not had an erection this side of the twentieth century . . .

Daisy, despite her girlish appearance, had been married for three years by 1942, ever since Sir Edward Gore-Allways had been recalled to his regiment in September 1939. It hadn't been the normal wartime marriage, so many of which had taken place that September. In her case she had thought that Teddy had made her pregnant; and as she had told her best friend Pamela Ponsonby, 'I know he's a dreadful old bore. All the same, he's got pots of money and I don't want to be left high and dry somewhere in the wolds of Gloucestershire, preggers, with the prospect of having to care for a little bastard for the rest of my born days.'

Accordingly a hasty marriage had been arranged, Teddy had gone off to France with his regiment and she had undergone a discreet abortion in an expensive London clinic, whereupon she had joined the Wrens and had begun to play the field. For Teddy was at least ten years older than she, a stick-in-the-mud sexually, and was quite content to rub himself off in the pair of silken French knickers ('black, please, Daisy, and worn at least once') that she had sent to him in France.

At first it had been young naval officers, who were jolly and high-spirited. But, as Daisy saw it, they had an unfortunate habit of going off up the Channel and getting themselves killed. Besides, most of them had only their pay to live off and Daisy had acquired expensive habits as the wife of a Guards officer of independent means. Then she had turned to foreign merchant skippers, running into the south coast harbours bringing supplies from the United States – they had plenty of black-market money selling their merchandise on the side. But mostly they were old and not very exciting. Thus, occasionally when she'd had a few too many G and Ts, she had indulged herself in a little rough trade: tough, virile men from the lower deck, especially the Americans, who had no particular sexual finesse but could make her twist and turn, squirming with passion, as they thrust themselves home inside her, calling her all the names under the sun as they did so. Lathered in sweat, her face red and ugly, she returned the sexual swear words, for she liked what she called to Pamela, 'Talking dirty. It makes me quite wet.'

It was in this manner she had acquired her taste for the Yanks, especially the Yankee soldiers, 'GIs' they called themselves, who were now appearing in London in ever-increasing frequency. She loved their uninhibited American manner. She knew they were coarse and vulgar sometimes and they chewed gum all the while like the animals back in the paddock at her Gloucestershire home. But they were so damned virile and they had no inhibitions about it. It was as if they hadn't had sex for months on end and could not get their fill of it now. On the nights and afternoons she could get away from her duties in Whitehall, she'd be off to the new American club or the American billets in Piccadilly, the former Splendide Hotel and the Badminton Club. She didn't mind their wolf whistles as they lounged against walls, chewing gum as usual. She liked the way they called to each other with what sounded like Red Indian war cries, or their organized baseball games in Green Park, where they drank beer out of what seemed to be tins and jeered the heavily armoured umpires. Everything about these fresh young men was delightful and as long as they were well supplied with 'rubbers' as they called their 'French letters', so that she didn't get 'preggers', she was quite prepared to satisfy their seemingly raging sexual appetites. Indeed, once she was half seas over, she had even entertained one of their 'dusky warriors', as she and her friend Pamela called the black GIs, in the bushes at the back of Green Park, while his comrades had been doing other kinds of press-ups under the supervision of their NCOs.

Now Daisy made her way into Piccadilly. It was getting close to blackout time and the area was already filled with the 'Piccadilly commandos' and even a few 'Hyde Park Rangers', who had strayed from their usual patch. Most of them were cheap whores, tottering on their high heels, their frocks poor quality and stained here and there by the misdirected efforts of their GI customers. But there were plenty of amateurs too. They had come into the city by train, selling their surburban bodies for the 'goodies', the 'Lucky Strikes', the 'Hershey Bars' and all the rest of those wonderful things with which the average American was supplied.

Daisy pretended not to notice either type. They were cheap and common – selling their working-class bodies, probably mostly unwashed, at a price. She, on the other hand, was doing it for something akin to love, well, at least sexual love.

Now as she strolled by 'Rainbow Corner' with the light vanishing progressively, she could hear the whores' cries: 'Hello soldier . . . Hello, dearie . . . Like a nice time, soldier . . . only ten bob, luv.' And always there'd be some GI who'd reply with what he thought was dashing wit, 'Honey, I don't want to *buy* it . . . just *rent* it that's all.'

She moved on down Shaftesbury Avenue towards the

Rainbow Corner Club, where she hoped her Wrens' uniform would get her into the all-American club. She'd done it before and she was sure she could do it again, for she liked the place. It epitomized America for her – from its barber shop to its jukeboxes. Besides, while the British pubs closed at ten in wartime, the Rainbow Club opened all night, offering hamburgers or American-type sandwiches to GIs who had no place to sleep.

She was right. Although the 'Piccadilly commandos' were kept at a distance by the US military policemen stationed outside, she was waved in with a wink by a cheerful young cop in his white helmet, who whispered, 'Good hunting, baby.'

To which she winked back and answered, 'Don't worry, corporal, about the hunting. I've always been good in the saddle!'

'I bet you have,' he said, as she went in, passing the sign over the reception desk stating 'New York – 3271 Miles'.

At this time of the evening, the place was humming. There were young soldiers and pretty girls everywhere. The very air seemed heavy with the heady odour of sex. She felt a tingling in her spine and even that familiar wetness between her legs of which she had spoken to the ancient colonel, although this time it was real.

She spotted him almost immediately. He was sitting by himself in one of the big easy chairs. But he wasn't slumped in the usual GI fashion; instead he was sitting upright, supporting himself with a stick, looking very trim and soldierly. Blond-headed, ruddy-complexioned, gleaming white teeth, the young American looked like one of those Hollywood stars that she had idolized before the war as a silly gushing, almost virginal girl.

He had spotted her, too. For he gave her the full benefit

of his dazzling smile and patted the seat of the chair next to him, as if indicating she should come and join him. She hesitated a mere moment. He had a stick of course and on his left breast he bore the purple square of the Purple Heart, which indicated that the handsome young American had been wounded. Later she wondered where, since as far as she knew the Americans hadn't been in action in Europe. But that was later. Despite being wounded, she could see by the look in his eyes that the GI had what it took; he'd be capable all right. And to judge by the prominent bulge in the front of his too tight khaki pants, he had more than enough to ensure that she was 'pleasured' in the manner she fancied. She hesitated no longer.

She crossed to the American, who was now making a gallant attempt to rise, with the aid of his cane. He smiled, displaying those well-cared-for, wonderful American teeth of his. She did the same, but carefully. British teeth, she had already learned, were never as good as US ones. 'Glad to meet you, miss,' he said. 'You look real swell in that Wren uniform.'

'Nice to meet you, too,' Daisy responded, and tried to return the compliment. 'And you look very fetching in that . . .' She broke off. She couldn't quite make out what branch of the US Army Forces the GI belonged to.

He saw her hesitation and his smile grew ever broader. 'We haven't been around too long, miss. So I'm not surprised you don't recognize my outfit.' He pointed to the green badge on his arm. 'I'm what you call a Ranger – Miss . . .'

# Two

Mackenzie had been sick twice. Major Dalby could understand why. The woman's corpse was a terrible sight. At first the two of them had not realized what they were going to be confronted with. Cherrill had not briefed them that well. The superintendent had stretched out his hand to encompass the bedroom and said, 'Little evidence of a struggle, eh, gentlemen?' And they had been forced to agree.

The place was sparse, save for the bed, a single straight-back chair, over which her clothing had been placed quite neatly, the khaki skirt concealing her issue knickers and ATS bra, with her shoes placed beneath it, her khaki stockings rolled neatly inside them.

But when the policeman had pulled back the shabby eiderdown and they had seen what lay beneath it, then Mackenzie had gagged and, with a muffled moan, had rushed to the landing toilet and been sick – violently. Hardly had he got back, face ashen and panting badly, as if he had just run a great race, than Cherrill had pointed to what had been taken out of her vagina, remarking, 'He did it with that screwdriver over in the sink,' and Mackenzie had stumbled out to be violently sick yet again.

The killer had thrust her on her face and stomach, raped her, tied up her hands behind her back with her ATS tie, gagged her too, and then, turning her over once more, had proceeded to carry out his terrible mutilations while she had still been alive, though as the pathologist (who had just left) had remarked, 'Thank God, the pain must have been so horrific that she passed out before he went very far. Let's hope anyway that was how it went.' He had departed, holding his handkerchief to his mouth and nose as if to ward off some terrible noxious odour.

Patiently the policeman waited till the younger Intelligence man had settled down before saying in his measured calm manner, as if he dealt with such terrible crimes every day of the week, 'Same pattern as before. A servicewoman, raped first and then mutilated. No attempt at robbery. Her handbag.' He indicated the khaki sling bag. 'Still got her money and leave ration book in it, even her fags – Woodbines,' he added, as if it was important.

'How do you mean – same pattern?' Dalby asked sharply.

By way of an answer, the policeman opened his big hand. There it was. That familiar arm patch of the US Rangers.

Dalby whistled softly. 'God in heaven!' he exclaimed. 'You mean we've got a barmy one on our hands?'

'Yes, murders according to a pattern, just like the Ripper.'

For a moment or two a heavy brooding silence followed and although Mackenzie was not a sensitive man – he didn't generally allow himself to be swayed by his imagination – now he did. He felt that the little bedroom, with that terrible, massacred corpse lying on the blood-soaked sheet in that pile of gore, had abruptly grown very cold. He shuddered in spite of himself. There was suddenly something very sinister and frightening about the place and he felt the sick bile rise in his throat once more. Christ, he wasn't going to make a fool of himself once more. No, he wasn't!

Hastily he cleared his throat and said, 'But what makes you think that, Super? I mean, this might be a copycat killing. Some madman reads or hears what happened to that other poor ATS and carries out a similar murder and mutilation. The world seems full of crazy people these days, including Adolf Hitler,' he added with a pale-faced attempt at humour.

The middle-aged policeman's face remained stoney. 'Agreed. There are plenty of loonies out there. I should know – I've met too many of the buggers in my police career. But how do you explain the Ranger patch?' He opened his hand again to reveal it. 'Where's your ordinary everyday looney going to get one of these? I mean, I'd never even heard of the Rangers till this business started.'

Dalby nodded sombrely. 'I understand. So if we're looking for your "looney" – a crazy fiend who rapes, murders and mutilates to a set pattern – we've got to look for someone who has access to these rare Ranger patches.'

'That's about it, Major,' the policeman agreed. He sighed as if he were abruptly very weary. 'The proof of the pudding will be the manner of the next murder . . .'

'Next murder!' Dalby echoed aghast. 'What do you mean?'

'Well, there will be one, you know, Major.'

'Why?'

'Because just like the Ripper taunted the police back in the last century, this killer is taunting us.'

'How do you mean, sir?' Mackenzie chimed, fascinated by the policeman's reasoning.

'Because he's giving us clues to his identity, making sure that we'll follow the trail till finally he's decided that he's played games long enough and, just as we're poised, or so we think, to strike and nab him, he does a bunk, just as the Ripper did. That's what all this "Ranger" stuff is about. He's leaving a calling card, as the Ripper did with his notes to Scotland Yard, and he's also told us that his victims are – and will be – servicewomen.'

'But it was said at the time,' Dalby objected, 'that the Ripper killed prostitutes because he hated them for some reason – perhaps they'd given him the pox – something like that. But we can't suppose that he hates servicewomen for a similar reason.'

'No, Major,' the policeman agreed. 'But he might just have a fetish for women in uniform, just like some blokes are excited by black underwear or women's high heels.'

Dalby frowned. He didn't like that sort of talk, Mackenzie knew. But it looked like his chief was going to have to face up to such issues while they were on this case. He said: 'So, according to your theories, Super: one, the killer will strike again; two, his victim will be another poor servicewoman?'

'Yes.'

'So what are we going to do about it, Super?' Dalby snapped, face stern and concerned. 'We can't just let another woman be murdered, and perhaps yet another, until this fiend gets tired of the sport and does a bunk, as you put it.'

'Of course not, sir,' the policeman agreed. 'But our resources are limited in the Met. Most of our younger men have been called up for the forces. We can't cover most of London as it is.'

'I can see that,' Dalby agreed. 'But while we're waiting, the criminal swine might well be lining up yet another unsuspecting girl for . . .' He didn't finish his sentence. But the two Intelligence officers read the policeman's mind. He was going to wait for the third victim to walk into the killer's trap and if the man's method of operation was the same as that of the previous two murders, then the middle-aged cop would know that he was dealing with a twentieth-century Ripper . . .

'But it's not moral,' Mackenzie objected hotly when they were thankfully outside and alone. 'We're just going to wait till some other young servicewoman's murdered!'

Down the street came a long column of German prisoners from the desert, escorted by a squad of middle-aged soldiers, their rifles slung over their shoulders, but with their bayonets fixed. Mostly they were from Rommel's *Afrikakorps* – the two officers could tell that by the peaked desert caps they wore at a jaunty angle. In contrast to their guards, they were bronzed, young and obviously very fit; indeed it was obvious to Dalby that they viewed their guards, probably from some home-service unit, with contempt.

'In this business, Mac,' Dalby said, not taking his gaze off the young German prisoners for a moment, 'we can't afford the luxury of morality.'

'But we can't sit on our thumbs and do nothing,' Mackenzie persisted.

'We won't. We'll recheck these Rangers without Truscott's aid, look into the deserter O'Corrigan more urgently. So far, since we published that thing about him, there's been no response.'

The sergeant in charge of the squad guarding the POWs came parallel with the officers. He was a little man, one of those fierce old sweats who were permanently tanned nut brown by the suns of the Empire. He probably hated the job he was doing as much as he hated the Jerries, Mackenzie thought to himself. Now he slammed his rifle down on his right shoulder smartly, raised his voice and barked in that high-pitched hysterical tone adopted by

Regular Army NCOs of his kind, 'Squad will march to
attention . . . Officer on parade . . . *Eyes right!*'

The squad obeyed correctly enough. Not the POWs from
the *Afrikakorps*.

They turned their heads lazily, even arrogantly, and
stared at the officer, who had clicked to attention in order
to return the squad's salute. A big blond *Gefreiter*, with
a coat over his arm and a heavy pack slung effortlessly
over his muscular shoulder, sneered, 'Ah, you English
gentlemen . . . At drill you are very good, eh . . . Not so
good at war. Cheerio, gentlemen . . . See you in Germany
soon . . . Then you will be our prisoners, no?' He waved
as if he really believed his statement, and went on his way
smiling.

'No talking in the ranks!' the sergeant rasped, face a
deep purple . . . '*Eyes front!*'

The column of prisoners marched on to their own dates
with destiny, leaving an angry fuming Dalby spluttering
with rage. 'My God, I could have let that arrogant Hun
swine have the back of my hand!' he cried, as their staff car
drew up slowly to take them back to Whitehall. 'God how I
hate to waste time on these sordid bloody murders when we
should be seeing how we can defeat those Hun bastards as
swiftly as possible. It's so damned frustrating.'

But sitting next to Mackenzie at the back of the big
khaki-painted Humber had calmed him down sufficiently
for him to order, 'We'll look into these Rangers without
Colonel Truscott's assistance this time. The War Office
can set it up for us. But our first priority is to nab this
deserter, the Irishman O'Corrigan.'

'Yessir,' Mackenzie agreed. 'He might be our man. His
record is full of acts of violence and he's regarded as
bolshy.' He hesitated momentarily. 'But somehow I can't
see him exactly as our murderer.'

'Neither can I, Mac. A man who's won a couple of good gongs like that and shed his blood for his country – no. Still, let's have a blitz on this one and get him into custody.'

'And you, sir?' Mackenzie enquired politely, watching as one of the barrage balloons which protected the capital against air attacks and which had broken loose, scudded across the blue sky like a fat silver elephant.

'There's another kind of flap on, Mackenzie.' Dalby lowered his voice in case the ATS driver was listening. 'The Rangers and the Commandos are going to go into action before the North Africa thing. I'll tell more details later. It's all very hush-hush and up in the air at the moment. I'll tell you this now, however, whatever transpires with this Ripper thing, we're going in with those Commandos.'*

Mackenzie whistled softly. 'Action again?'

'Action again,' Dalby echoed as they drew into White-hall and the immaculate Royal Marine sentries pulled aside the barbed-wire barriers and checked their identity cards before letting them proceed. 'And remember this, Mac, our time is running out fast, very fast.'

Major Dalby didn't know just how fast it was running out for him . . .

A mile or so away, the wounded Ranger, helped by Daisy, made his way slowly up the dim blue-lit stairs of the big boarding house. At least he had told her it was a boarding house. She, however, had other ideas about the place, for she sensed it was mostly occupied by single Yanks and the kind of cheap tarts that they picked up. From the left, on the landing, there came the muted sound of panting and the accompanying squeaking of rusty bedsprings. From

* See L. Kessler: *Murder at Colditz* (Severn House) for further details.

the right, a gramophone was playing the inane jingle of that year, '*Mairzy Doats and Doazy Doats and liddle Lamzy tivey . . . A kiddley tivey too, wouldn't you . . .?*' But the purpose the place was being used for didn't worry Daisy. Indeed it made her excited. She felt that familiar tingling again and when he had supposedly accidentally bumped into her right breast as they had mounted the tight stairs, her nipple had grown as hard as a rock at once. She said to herself, 'I hope he tries it on tonight . . . I'd just love a good poke.'

Surprisingly enough the tall wounded Ranger, who said she should call him Rick, hadn't started pawing her immediately, as she had expected. Instead he had seated her very courteously in front of the flickering gas fire and had made a decent stiff G and T while he'd drunk something called 'Coke'. She believed it was a soft drink or something like that. She told herself he wanted to get her drunk before he tried to get his hand up her knickers. She hoped so at least.

She was disappointed. He wasn't the usual American, who could hardly get his pants off quickly enough. Naturally she could see that he was sexually attracted to her; she was well experienced in such matters. Constantly he touched that bulge in the front of his tight-fitting trousers, as if to reassure himself that his penis was still there. But his conversation was free of sexual innuendo, and he seemed concerned to talk about Minnesota, from whence he came, and that 'good, old-time religion', as he phrased it: something which bored her stiff.

After half an hour or so and three stiff gins, with the light fading rapidly outside, so that she knew it would soon be time to put up the blackout, she was beginning to wonder if the handsome blond brute opposite her was a pansy. There were plenty of them in London and in the easier conditions of wartime they were flaunting their perversion; but she'd never met an American one before. Daisy, as bold as always, decided the time had come to discover what made this 'Ranger', as he called himself, tick. She took another hefty swig of her G and T, reached over for the pack of Camels he had opened for her – 'I never touch tobacco,' he had told her, 'you have to avoid, when you can, the Devil's temptations' – and at the same time carelessly opened her legs.

That did it.

But not in the manner she had anticipated exactly.

He turned slowly, and later, she realized, very slowly, as if he were wondering whether he should continue in what he was going to do, and then headed to the little makeshift kitchen at the back of the room, separated from it by a dirty flowered curtain. She sat there, legs still apart, numbed a little by the gin, wondering if he were going to prepare her another drink. For a few moments, she couldn't take in and identify the strange sound coming from the other room. It was a strange scraping noise.

An instant later she knew to her shocked horror what it was. The curtain was thrust back and there he was. He had removed his trousers and she could see the angry red marks of his wounded legs and the great club-like erection that he bore in front of him like a priest carrying a chalice.

But it wasn't the erection that attracted the attention of her overheated, slightly drunken gaze, it was the knife he bore in his upraised hand, his teeth bared like those of some wild animal ready to spring on its unsuspecting prey.

# Three

Mackenzie settled back in the solitary comfort of the first-class compartment. As usual in wartime, the train heading south-west to the naval ports was packed with servicemen and women. They crowded the corridor outside, throwing envious glances and some of wonder at this lone sergeant in the Intelligence Corps with his packet of bully beef sandwiches on the empty seat next to him, trying to work out how such a low-ranking 'brown job' could get a reserved compartment to himself.

Twice after stops, suspicious military policemen had boarded the train and, after hesitating at the reserved sign on the door of Mackenzie's compartment, stamped by the London RTO, had slid the door open and commanded, 'Can I see yer pass, Staff, and your travel permit?' While one of them had examined the documents, the other, in typical redcap fashion, had eyed Mackenzie up and down, checking whether he could find something wrong with him that might lead to further examination or even to arrest. Twice the military police had failed, for Mackenzie was well versed in such matters. NCOs travelling first-class were always objects of suspicion. And he knew, if the worst came to the worst, he had a single sheet of typed paper with that great sprawled signature at its base that would awe even a field marshal.

It was Dalby who had sent him on this hurried mission,

while he urged the police and the London Military Police Provost Marshal to redouble their efforts to find the deserter, O'Corrigan; and attend to his own mysterious mission soon to come. After handing him that all-important document, hurriedly dispatched from Number Ten Downing Street, he had said, 'Let's make a new start on those Rangers – oh, and by the way, Mac, see if you can talk *privately* to O'Corrigan's platoon sergeant, this Sergeant Hawkins. Those infantry NCOs might not be the brightest—' Hastily he excused himself with, 'I know . . . I know, Mac. You're a non-com yourself.'

'Ours is to obey, sir. You know what we lowly other ranks say, "If it moves salute it, if it don't, paint it." That is our task in life.' He grinned. Momentarily Dalby had shared his grin before becoming serious once more and ending his briefing with, 'See, too, what you can find out about this Ranger, Larsen, who was hospitalized after the incident with the grenade—'

Mackenzie had interrupted him with a quick, 'Larsen seems to have discharged himself from the hospital. The people at the Army General didn't know quite what to do about it. They had no jurisdiction over Larsen, as he was an American soldier, the first they'd ever treated. So they let him draw all his back pay through the Field Cashier and off he went.'

'Where?' Dalby had asked, glancing at his watch, as if he were in a great hurry.

'God knows. I got Field Security to try to trace his movements. They came up with a blank, but I think he must have headed for the Smoke. Every serviceman does when he gets the chance. You know, wine, women and song, sir.'

'I don't know about that, Mac. Remember my age. At my age the only thing left is the wine.' He had tapped his pocket which contained the silver flask, filled with scotch and which Mac thought his boss was drinking too much of these days.

But there had been no time for such considerations. Half an hour later Mac was seated in his plush first-class compartment with the faded pre-war photos of the south-western holiday resorts on the walls, his sandwiches on the seat next to him, plus the folder of papers that a motorcycle messenger from Scotland Yard had delivered to him at the station.

Now Mackenzie was getting sick of the stares coming from the packed corridor – a Wren had even stuck her tongue out at him. So, he picked up the folder from the Superintendent at Scotland Yard and took out one of his thick wads and started to read. *Jack the Ripper*, it began.

> For three months from the end of August to the beginning of November in the Year of 1888, the Whitechapel area of London bore witness to a series of vicious murders. The slayings were characterized by unparalleled savagery. Each of the five victims, all common prostitutes, had been attacked from behind and their throats cut from ear to ear. In four of the cases the bodies were subsequently subjected to mutilation and dissection. This suggested a perverted sexual motive . . .

Normally Mackenzie enjoyed the wads served by the cookhouse, especially the ones containing corned beef and not the usual dry old cheese. But now, suddenly, he lost his taste for bully beef, even though on this occasion the cook who had made up his 'haversack ration', had smeared brown sauce liberally on the tinned meat. He put the half-eaten wad back on the seat next to him, watched greedily by the pretty young Wren who had stuck her tongue out at him.

He cleared his abruptly dry throat and with an effort of will, continued to read, knowing already that there would be worse to come. There was.

*The first victim*, the Scotland Yard report continued,

> was Mary Ann Nichols (called 'Polly'), who perished on Friday 31 August 1888 in Buck's Row. A police report on the following morning stated, 'No murder was ever more ferociously and more brutally done.' Eight days later 'Dark Annie' Chapman, forty-five years of age, was slaughtered in a similarly vicious manner in Hanbury Street.
>
> On 30 September, the murderer went even further. He committed a double murder. The first body was found at approximately one o'clock in the morning in Berner Street. The body was that of a woman with a deep gash that ran from ear to ear. Later she was identified as 'Long Liz' Stride. Some hours later the second body was discovered in the corner of Mitre Square. It was that of Catherine Eddowes. In this case the face had been so brutally slashed that it was exceedingly hard to identify her. In addition the abdomen had been ripped open and a portion of her intestines had been dragged out and left draped around the dead woman's neck. It was suggested at the time that this was 'the work of a practised hand'.

Mackenzie gulped, fighting off the hot bile which threatened to choke him. In the corridor the cheeky young Wren, a mere girl really, had pulled up her tight navy-blue skirt to reveal the white thigh above the black stocking top. She was licking her lips and indicating the half-eaten sandwich, smiling winningly. For a moment Mackenzie was tempted; she was such a pretty young girl in her smart blue uniform. Then he thought of the paper he was reading. He shook his head and bent down to the gruesome account once more. The girl's smile vanished. She dropped her skirt and began to sulk. Mackenzie let her. The very thought of sex, after what he had just read, revolted him, made him ashamed of being a man with all the normal young man's sexual drives.

He turned to the last of the Ripper's murders; the attack on Mary Jane Kelly in her room at Miller's Court on the night of 9 November 1888. The original report didn't spare any of the terrible details of what the loathsome creature had done to the Irish whore. It was only by a sheer effort of willpower that Mackenzie could bring himself to continue reading. *The throat had been cut*, the fifty-four-year-old report read,

> right across with a knife, nearly severing the head from the body. The abdomen had been partially ripped open and both of the breasts had been cut from the body; the left arm, like the head, hung from the body by the skin only. The nose had been cut off, the forehead skinned and the thighs had been slashed with a knife across and downwards. The liver and entrails had been wrenched away. The entrails and other portions of the frame were missing, but the liver etc. were found placed between the feet of the poor victim. The flesh from the thighs and legs, together with the breasts and nose, had been placed by the murderer on the table and one of the hands of the dead woman had been pushed into her stomach—

Mackenzie stopped. He could read no more. If he did he knew he would be sick. With hands that trembled badly, he opened a packet of Players and took out a cigarette with great difficulty. At the same time, he called for the young Wren to come in. He had to talk with someone normal. He couldn't stand being alone to consider the dreadful things he had just read.

She came in at a hurry. She slumped down with a weary sigh. 'Thank God, Staff. I've been on the road since York. My legs are killing me. And I'm hungry.' She eyed the half-eaten bully-beef sandwich pointedly. 'Take a fresh one,' he said. 'From the haversack. There's a plum-jam one if you want something sweet.'

'Ta very much.' She grabbed the sandwich as if she hadn't eaten for days and took a great bite at the thick wad. 'Got anything to drink, Staff?' she asked, her pretty little mouth full of jam and bread. 'Fair clemmed, I am.'

'There's some tea in the thermos.'

'Anything stronger?' she asked, chewing mightily.

Mackenzie was just about to tell her there wasn't; then he remembered the half a bottle of Haig that he had been going to give his boss for his birthday, but hadn't when he realized just how much Major Dalby was drinking these days. 'There's some whisky in the haversack. But I don't suppose you drink the hard stuff. At your age—'

'My age!' she interrupted him with a knowing wink. 'I thought you was in the Intelligence Corps. Where's you bin these last few years? Natch, I drink whisky, though I wouldn't mind a drop o' tap water in it so that it ain't so strong.'

'Of course,' he said, dazed a little still. He unscrewed the cap of the thermos and opened the door of the compartment. 'Half a mo.'

The 'half a mo' turned out to be five minutes, the corridor

was that crowded, including the lavatory, where a sailor was sitting on the seat with a Wren on his knee, both of them red-faced and drunk, waving bottles of Light Brown Ale, singing away lustily about *'up came the spider, sat down beside her and whipped his old bazooka out . . . Get hold o' this, get hold o' that . . . Big balls, small balls, balls as big as yer head . . .'* It took some time to persuade them to stop singing and fill his cup. When they did and he got back to his compartment, he found the Wren had had a shot of the whisky without water and had pulled down the leather blinds of the compartment, saying, as she held up her black knickers, 'Lock the door, Staff, it's your lucky day.' She giggled like a silly little schoolgirl.

He did so, realizing that she wasn't really used to drink. So he said, 'If you have another one, dear, you'll feel it.'

She giggled again and answered, 'If I have another one, I'll feel it for you. Come on, pour me a real drink and sit down beside me, if you don't mind sitting next to a daft lass from Yorkshire, you and your Intelligence Corps.'

For some reason, he didn't feel insulted by the reference; indeed, he felt for her. She was just another girl caught up in a great war, who would undoubtedly never get over the experience; she was one of those who would be doomed to be a victim of the conflict. A few minutes later he realized that he was right. She had another quick drink of the Haig – 'Don't be vague, order Haig,' as she giggled – and another. Then to his complete surprise, she was fumbling drunkenly with his flies. He was too flabbergasted to stop her. But the surprises didn't end there.

She made him excited and then, slipping awkwardly out of her shoes, she knelt before him, muttering, 'Stand by to repel boarders.' Next moment, she had taken his penis into her mouth, swallowing the full length of it so that whatever else she said as she did so was choked.

For one second he was tempted to push her head away. Why should she carry out this perverted act on him, a complete stranger? It wasn't right. She was just a kid. But just for a moment. The sheer pleasure of this unnatural sex swept all moral inhibitions to one side. Now all he wanted was to enjoy. He seized both sides of her head and forced her downwards, groaning with the joy of it all.

Even so that bit of Shakespeare he had learned as a callow youth swept into his mind, blotting out the thoughts of what the nineteenth-century Ripper had done to his victims. 'Love is merely a madness; and, I tell you, deserves as well a dark house and a whip as madmen do; and the reason why they are not so punished and cured is that the lunacy is so ordinary that the whippers are in love, too.'

Then he was pumping his erection into her mouth, not caring any more about her youth and perhaps innocence, concerned only with his own pleasure, mouthing foul curses and urgent orders till finally his spine curved like a taut bow and, completely isolated in a frenetic world of his own, he let go . . .

He got off at Kingsbridge. She was pretty drunk still but walked to the door with him. Now she was sad and thoughtful though. As he got down to the platform and saw the Commando sergeant marching across to pick him up from the station, she said, recognizing the insignia, 'So you're with them, are you?' She gave him a sad smile. 'Well look after yourself when you go . . . Don't get yersen bloody killed.' Then she turned and the steel wheels of the long train clattered as the engine started to pull it forward. She didn't look back.

It was only later that a pensive Mackenzie realized two things. One, that she knew about this mysterious future operation and, two, he didn't even know her name . . .

'Sergeant Hawkins, Staff, Commando Brigade,' the little bandy-legged NCO, with the respectful but wary face of an old sweat, reported as Mackenzie passed through the ticket barrier, carrying his bag. Out of the corner of his eye he noted the two redcaps sitting in their jeep, keeping their hard gazes on the travellers passing through with him. That surprised him – MPs at this remote little station – but he made no comment, as the little Commando sergeant said, 'The brigade major sent me to fetch you, Staff. I've got a fifteen-hundredweight van just behind the station.'

'Good of him!' Mackenzie commented, wondering if he might tackle the sergeant about the Rangers. He looked the type who would note everything. All the same, he also looked as if he wouldn't be given to gossip.

'When the major heard you was from Intelligence, he nearly shat hissen,' Hawkins answered. 'He thought you might be trouble. So he's laying out the red carpet, including me, for yer.' He winked.

Mackenzie winked back. One thing was established already, he thought, Sergeant Hawkins didn't like the brigade major.

Five minutes later they were heading for the coast, past a column of tall lanky Americans, who looked totally unlike the overfed, lazy types that Mackenzie had seen so far in the Smoke. These men were doing a speed march, laden down with their heavy weapons and in full battle order. But despite the fact they were crimson-faced with the effort and sweating like pigs, they were bearing up well. Hawkins saw the direction of his gaze and said, 'We're giving 'em a sort of rest day today. Taking it easy like.'

Mackenzie grinned. 'If you call that taking it easy, Sarge.' He shrugged. 'By the way, you can call me Mac, if you like.'

'What an honour, *Mac*,' Hawkins said and for a moment

100

concentrated on avoiding a Ranger officer who was trailing behind the column, carrying his own rifle and a BAR light machine gun that he had taken from one of his men, who was fading a bit. Then he said, 'Is it Mr O'Corrigan, Mac? Is that why you've put the shits up the brigade major, cos he knows that if they ever return the lieutenant to the brigade, he'll have the brigade major's guts for garters, that's for certain.'

'In a way,' Mac answered carefully, 'and also to get a bit o' info on the Yanks.'

Hawkins tugged his nose, as if he were giving the matter some thought. 'On the whole they're good lads. They're all volunteers and they're willing horses. 'Course, they're full of themselves, shooting off their mouths and such like. But I've heard all Yanks is like that, Mac.' He shot Mackenzie a look, but the latter didn't respond. He wanted the little brown-faced NCO to keep on talking.

'The only one I don't like – *didn't*,' he corrected himself quickly, 'is that yellow-haired basket who did for Mr O'Corrigan.'

'You mean Ranger Larsen?'

'Yer. Swede, the others called him. That's him.'

'I know about the grenade incident. But why didn't you like him personally?'

''Cos he was bloody strange, that's why, Mac. In one way he was a bit of a Holy Joe, all that religion stuff, trying to shove it down the other blokes' throats, and they didn't like it either. And on the other, he was a real sex fiend.'

'Go on,' Mackenzie urged, his attention captured now.

'Yer, allus playing with hissen, as if he was wanking. Then it was all the bints he'd rogered. Cor, ferk a duck, Mac, he was always on about it. What he'd done to 'em and how they were nearly begging for him to stick 'em a link. Put a bloke off the other, I can tell yer.' He spat

101

out of the open window in disgust. 'But one thing I can tell yer, Mac, about his nibs, which really got yours truly thinking hard.'

'And what's that?' Mackenzie asked eagerly.

'This.' The little sergeant changed down swiftly as they started to enter the little side road leading to the cliff-top Commando camp. 'One night me and Mr O'Corrigan was on orderly officer duty and we came across this Larsen bloke in the bogs.'

'Yes?'

'And he was stark bollock-naked, weeping and wailing and praying to frigging heaven – the whole Holy Joe lot. Mr O'Corrigan said we wasn't to disturb him. But after we went off duty next morning, instead of getting into me wanking pit for a bit o' kip, I went back to the bogs to have a proper look-see by daylight. And d'yer know what I found there, Mac?'

Mackenzie shook his head as the van pulled up in front of the headquarters office. 'Blood . . . dry, congealed blood. Now what d'yer make of that, eh, mate?'

But at that particular moment, Mackenzie could not make anything of it whatsoever, save to tell himself that this Ranger, Larsen, had to be brought in for questioning pretty damned quick.

# Four

Daisy came to with a groan. For one long moment she thought she had awoken from a heavy sleep, troubled by bad dreams. Then she felt the burning pain in her right hand. She looked down. Through eyes blackened and swollen to narrowed slits, she saw the deep bright-red gashes on the palm. Then it all came back to her: the crazy American with his great erection bobbing up and down in front of her, the upraised knife, the blood shining on the blade in the light of the single bulb, the gross obscenities he was shouting at her. For a second or two she had lain on the floor, petrified with fear. But then reason and a wild fury had taken possession of her. She was not just going to lie there and allow herself to be slaughtered like some dumb, tame beast. She was going to fight back.

In the same instant that he bent over her, his face contorted with foam and spittle spraying from his lips as he threatened her with what he was going to do to her once he had 'ripped those panties off that disgusting smelly cunt of yours, bitch!' she lashed out her right foot. The blow caught him right in the crotch. He stumbled back, his erection vanished in a flash, the knife lowered, as he started to retch.

Daisy hadn't given him a chance to recover. Trying not to feel the terrible pain in her lacerated hands, she stumbled to the door, blood dripping in great red gobs from her wounded palms. It was locked. She almost panicked. Behind her, he was recovering. 'Don't open that door, whore!' he commanded thickly. She was not listening. Clumsily, her hands greasy with her own blood, she fumbled with the key.

He was coming towards her again, knife upraised once more. He stumbled against a chair. It crashed to the floor. From below some American shouted, 'Hey, what the Sam Hill's going on up there?' He didn't seem to hear. He raised the knife higher. In a moment he'd bring the razor-sharp blade down into her back.

The lock snapped open. With the rest of her strength, she tugged the door open. He slammed into the wall. Next instant she was clattering down the stairs, screaming at the top of her voice, but knowing at the same time she wasn't going to last much longer. She could already feel herself weakening from the loss of blood.

Somehow she tumbled down the stairs and out into the blacked-out street. Behind her the house was in an uproar. Dimly she heard women screaming and American GIs cursing angrily. But only dimly. She shook her head, as a thick black mist threatened to overcome her. Her vision cleared for a few seconds. In the blue light from the hall lamp, she caught a glimpse of the basement garden, a pile of rubbish and weeds really. She was tempted. But she knew instinctively that would be the first place the monster would look for her; and already she could hear him clattering down the stairs, panting like some predatory animal eager for prey, shouting excitedly when, it seemed, someone might bar his progress.

'Oh, my God!' Daisy said to herself. 'What am I to do?' For she knew she was weakening by the instant. She'd black out soon. But by then she had to be under cover, hidden. For she knew he wouldn't spare her. Even now he'd slash her to death to keep her from talking.

She held on to the wall, feeling her way weakly like a blind woman. Then she spotted what she sought – a large ashcan. Once in some comic film or other she had seen someone hide in an ashcan. Now there was nothing comic about her predicament. She had to find cover – *at once*.

Feeling herself fading rapidly, she had pulled out the rubbish in the ashcan and had scrambled the best she could inside, pulling the lid in after her. Then she heard him: 'Where are you, bitch?' he was growling. 'Come on, I'm going to find you sooner or later. Better let it happen now and get it over with.' He laughed like a maniac. 'Perhaps yer gonna like it—'

Somewhere a whistle had shrilled urgently. That did it. In the same instant that she fainted, she heard him curse, 'Sonovabitch!' and then there was the sound of running feet and she had known no more . . .

It had taken what seemed an age for her to get out of the ashcan. The effort had been a tremendous strain, her hands were bleeding heavily and she couldn't get a grip on the side of the ashcan to lever herself out. She had fainted again and had felt herself falling to the ground. Now she was coming to once more, realizing again the full horror of what had happened to her. For a few moments she simply slumped there, gasping for breath, as if she had just run a great race. Then she realized she had first to do something about her right hand, which was still bleeding very badly. She had learned enough in the Wrens first-aid classes to know that she could bleed to death here on the damp flags if she didn't do something soon. Then the shrilling of the whistle penetrated her consciousness. Her thought processes seemed to have slowed a lot. It was a long time, or so she thought later, until she realized who would have blown that whistle. 'Police,' she gasped weakly. She raised herself on one elbow, her head already spinning again.

'Over here,' she called in a cracked voice. 'Police, over—'
The words died on her lips . . .

'So you thought you were gonna escape, cunt, eh?' the
GI sneered, appearing out of nowhere, towering above her,
that terrible, blood-dripping knife raised, ready to strike
once more. 'Well, you're wrong. You're gonna die – and
then some, baby.'

'No, no!' she pleaded. She raised one hand to shield
her face, feeling the great gobs of hot blood from the
lacerations dripping on to her skin. 'Please, don't . . . I
won't tell,' she quavered in her absolute terror. 'You can
still get away . . .'

'*Fuck you!*' he grated through clenched teeth as he prepared to bring down that savage final blow. '*Die, bitch!*'

She gave one last scream and then everything went a
merciful black and she knew no more . . .

The brigade major had blustered and been his usual supercilious self. O'Corrigan had got what he deserved. He had
been a bolshy insubordinate officer, who had thought he
could do just what he pleased because he'd won a good
gong in the Middle East. As for talking to the American
Rangers, he was training them, but he didn't feel he could
allow Mackenzie to talk to them individually. That was
in the jurisdiction of their commander, Colonel Truscott.
Besides, there was an op being planned – very hush-hush.
He didn't feel that a mere staff sergeant, even if he was
in the 'green slime' – the brigade major had meant the
Intelligence Corps – should be privy to such matters . . .

Mackenzie had let him ramble on for a while, still
standing to attention in front of the brigade major, as if he
were a raw recruit, until he could tolerate the monologue
no longer. With a polite, 'Sir, can I stop you for a moment?'
he had caught the officer totally by surprise.

'Stop me? How do you mean, Staff Sergeant?' he had demanded.

By way of an answer Mackenzie had reached in the breast pocket of his battledress blouse and brought out the precious handwritten document that Dalby had given him before he had left London. He handed it to the self-important major with, 'Perhaps you'd care to read that, sir.'

'Why the devil should I?' the former had snorted. He waved the letter to one side.

Mackenzie stuck to his guns. 'I think you ought to, sir. It's in your own best interest.'

Something in Mackenzie's manner must have convinced him for he had said grudgingly, 'Oh well, give the damned thing here.'

He unfolded the note impatiently and stopped short when he saw the letterhead. 'This is from the Cabinet Office,' he gasped.

Feeling no sense of triumph at the sight of the major seemingly shrunken like a balloon suddenly deflated, Mackenzie had answered, 'Yessir. It's from the Prime Minister, Mr Churchill.' He didn't look directly at the major, but continued to stare at some distant object over the major's shoulder, as a good, well-disciplined soldier should.

By the time he had finished reading the note, in which Churchill made it clear that Staff Sergeant Mackenzie should be given every possible aid 'without let or hindrance', the self-important brigade major's attitude had changed completely. Now he was deferential, almost toadylike. Thus it was that Mackenzie had been able to question the Rangers individually, guided by Sergeant Hawkins, who was obviously well liked by the Rangers, all a head taller than the little old sweat.

It didn't take Mackenzie long to discover that Larsen had been heartily disliked by his comrades. Not only had he been disliked, he had also been an object of bewilderment and suspicion. 'Holy roller type,' they commented. 'All that holy, holy, holy crapula.' 'Yeah, and at the same time,' others said, 'he was always shooting off his mouth about all the dames he'd laid back in the States.'

'Yeah,' another Ranger had chimed in. 'Yet when we get to North Ireland, he wouldn't have no truck with them Irish broads. Said they was all Papists and whores! He really went on about them Mick B-girls.'

That evening in the sergeant's mess, having a couple of 'wets', as Hawkins called the pints of beer, the latter said, 'Our friend Larsen's turning out to be a bit of a funny sod, ain't he, Mac?'

Mackenzie was forced to agree. He said, 'Yes, the women and the boasting and then this hatred of the pros and the Catholics. It could mean something.'

Hawkins nodded, taking his eyes off his fellow sergeants making a great fuss of their darts and the wagers they were making about who'd get the first bullseye. 'They're all a funny lot really,' Hawkins said apropos of nothing.

'Who are?'

'The Yanks are, of course. They're not bad lads. They have tried bloody hard while they've been here.' It was only later that Mackenzie remarked upon that past tense – 'have tried' – as if the Rangers' time at the Commando camp was over. 'Of course, most of them'll get killed. They're too full of themsens. When it comes to it and the shit is flying, they'll all try to be frigging heroes and have their frigging heads blown off. That's what happens to heroes.' Hawkins took a moody sip of the warm beer.

Mackenzie laughed sympathetically. 'You don't like them much, do you?'

'In a way I do. They're bloody generous with their stuff. But they've got such big mouths. The way they go on about America and the frigging American way of life, whatever that is when it's at home. We're *quaint*, you know, Mac.' He said the word as if it were disgusting. '*Olde worlde* and all that, *plucky little Britain*! They don't realize we've been fighting for our frigging lives for years. But it don't matter. They'll sort it out for us. The Yanks are here. Nuthin' can go wrong now.'

Mackenzie was tempted to enter a discussion with the little old sweat on the subject of Americans and the Brave New World they planned for Britain, whether Britain liked it or not. But he didn't have the time. This business with 'Swede' Larsen was too pressing. So he said: 'Anything else to report about the Yank?'

'Just this.' Hawkins forgot his moans about the Yanks. Then he told Mackenzie about the episode with the blood once more and what he had found during the course of the day after questioning two of the Rangers who had served with him in the US 34th Infantry Division in Northern Ireland before they had volunteered for the Rangers. 'You know what sheep mutilation is, don't yer, Mac?' Hawkins asked.

'Well, I understand the words,' Mackenzie answered, puzzled at the direction of the conversation. 'But I don't understand exactly what you mean by them.'

'You'll just have to grow up, Mac. You know you get to one of them remote postings and there's no womenfolk around and a bloke gets randy and he gets desperate and on a Saturday night he gets a skinful of booze and one thing leads to another and if the bloke's from the country and knows about them things, off he goes into the stables and . . . Well, come on Mac, you're in the bloody Intelligence Corps, use yer bloody intelligence.' Hawkins stopped the long monologue and looked at Mackenzie almost accusingly.

Momentarily Mackenzie's mouth dropped open when he realized what the little old sweat was saying. 'Oh, my God, you mean—'

'Yes, I do mean it. That's what I got from them two other Rangers and they were pretty embarrassed and ashamed of having to tell me it. Besides, they thought Larsen had brought shame on the Rangers and they would have reported him, but they didn't know what really to say.' He laughed grimly and took a hefty swig at his beer. 'I mean, you can expect that sort o' thing happening to squaddies stationed in the Shetlands, but not in Ireland where there's plenty of willing bints, professional or otherwise. But that's not the end of it.'

This time it was Mackenzie's turn to take a deep drink of his beer. 'Go on,' he said grimly. 'Tell me the worst.'

'It was the sheep, as I've just said, Mac. Well, it was about that time that the Red Bulls, that's what the Yanks of the 34th Div called themselves – they would, wouldn't they, being Yanks.'

'Get on with it,' Mackenzie urged, wanting and yet not wanting to know the worst.

'Out on exercises, they started coming across the carcasses of sheep. I'd better not tell yer exactly what had been done to 'em, you being a delicate sort o' feller. Suffice to say, Mac, they were all mutilated. Very nasty indeed. Before the local rozzers could investigate who done it, the Ranger volunteers were posted to here. But I don't think yer need a crystal ball to guess who the main suspect was . . .'

But Mackenzie was no longer listening to Sergeant Hawkins. He knew enough now.

Over at the sergeant's mess dartboard a big Marine sergeant with an upswept moustache, who would be dead before this month was out, was shouting triumphantly, 'Will yer get yer glassy orbits on that, mates. A double bullseye! Who's paying for the wallop now, eh?'

*Yes*, Mackenzie told himself, *a double bullseye indeed*. He'd got him. He'd got Ranger 'Swede' Larsen.

Five minutes later he was telephoning Major Dalby at the War Ministry in London telling him his exciting news. In return Dalby had similar news for him. 'They've found a girl – a Wren to be exact. Another victim. But this one survived. She's in a very bad way, but we think she'll pull through. And –' he emphasized the words – 'she can identify the man who attacked her. It's the same one.' He let the news sink in, then he said, urgency in his voice, 'Tie up the loose ends and then get back to London as soon as possible. We'll wind up this dreadful case and after that –' he hesitated only an instant, knowing this was an open line which could be tapped – 'the op I told you about is on. We are as well.' The line went dead.

# Five

T he US assistant military attaché from the embassy placed his hand on Larsen's broad shoulder and said, 'Now don't you worry, soldier. Just tell the truth and it'll be OK with the limeys. They don't want to upset the apple cart, especially now as the Rangers are going on their first mission in the European theatre of operations.'

'Yessir,' Larsen answered quietly. He was dressed in his Class-A uniform with the square ribbon of the Purple Heart on his chest, clean-shaven, hair freshly cut and well parted. Indeed he looked like the ideal US soldier, as depicted on the US Army recruiting posters back home. It was not surprising. PFC Larsen had been groomed specifically by the embassy staff, on orders from no less a person than General Marshall, the US chief of staff back in Washington. Just like Churchill, the crusty head of the US Army wanted no problems with the new Anglo-American relationship that Churchill had worked so hard to achieve.

'Yessir, Major,' Larsen answered quietly. 'I will tell the truth. If I swear on the Good Book, I mean it, sir. That's the way I was brought up to be.'

'That's the style, son,' the assistant military attaché said enthusiastically. He liked a soldier who believed in the Bible.

At the end of the long corridor, smelling of ether, Harpic and human misery, the constable on guard outside Wren

Daisy's room beckoned. In a whisper, he said, 'They'll see you soon.' He saluted and the attaché acknowledged the salute with a gruff, 'Thank you, officer.' He propelled Larsen forward. 'Come on, son, the sooner we get it over with the better.'

The orderly in the white coat who had been watching the pair for the last five minutes suddenly decided, it seemed, that the show was over. He started to push the wheelchair towards the lift. The constable on guard dismissed him from his field of observation.

The white-painted hospital room was crowded when the two Americans entered. There were the two Intelligence men, a representative from the War Office, Colonel Truscott, and a civilian who might have come from Number Ten; he hadn't introduced himself, but obviously he was that important that he hadn't been checked by Superintendent Cherrill, who was standing by the bed of the most important person there, 'Wren Daisy'.

The Super took over immediately while Dalby and Mackenzie watched him intently. 'We're here for – er – Wren Daisy to make a possible identification,' he started in a no-nonsense businesslike manner. 'No one has legal representation. None is needed until a formal charge is made.' By the look on Cherrill's face as he stared hard at the big American Ranger it was clear to Mackenzie at least, that the policeman was prepared to make that formal charge soon. 'Will you step forward more into the light, Ranger?'

Slowly Larsen did so and Mackenzie noted his feet seemed to be hurting him, though his broad handsome face revealed nothing save that he saw himself as someone who was completely innocent and was here because of some grave mistake.

The policeman nodded to the young nurse with the red

cross painted on the front of her white starched overall. Gently she cradled the Wren's upper body in her arms and raised her. Despite the hospital treatment, Daisy looked a sorry mess. Both her eyes were still narrowed to slits, her cheeks were green and blue and bruised while her hands were both swathed in heavy bandages.

Mackenzie and Dalby looked grim. They knew the Wren was going to find it hard to overcome her ordeal and identify the Ranger in the condition she was in. Besides, the assistant military attaché, who, according to Colonel Truscott, was representing not only the Pentagon, but the President himself, would challenge any positive identification even if Daisy managed it, saying she was too shocked and ill to be able to recognize Larsen as her attacker.

But none of them had reckoned with Daisy's spirit and intelligence. She peered at Larsen through her half-closed eyes, but then instead of saying that he was the culprit, she asked, 'Make him speak. Can I have him speak?'

'Speak?' the Super echoed, surprised, as they all were.

'Yes, please, make him say these words. "Fuck you . . . die, bitch".'

There was a shocked gasp from the men present and the young nurse's hand flew to her mouth in surprise. All of them were hard, used to the violence and even death of wartime England, but these obscenities coming from the injured girl shook them.

For a moment there was a heavy silence. Then the US military attaché protested, 'You can't have Ranger Larsen say such words . . . Why, he's a very religious man. His father's a preacher back home.'

The Super recovered first. It was clear from the look in his hard eyes that he knew that Daisy had identified the wartime Ripper. It was Larsen all right and he was not going to let him get away just on account of a few crude Anglo-Saxon terms. 'Say it . . . Say the words,' he ordered, ignoring the red-faced military attaché. 'Come on now. We've not got all the time in the world, and if you're bashful, we'll get you a preacher afterwards to absolve you – or would soap and water to wash your mouth out be better for you?'

Larsen flushed. He moved a little closer. He looked appealingly at the attaché. He affected not to notice. The matter was out of his hands. Larsen gave a little shrug and cleared his throat. There was deathly silence in the hospital room now. All eyes were fixed on the handsome blond Ranger.

'F—' he commenced, as if his throat was abruptly constricted. 'Fuck you.' His face flushed an even deeper red. '*D . . . die . . . bitch.*' He choked on the last word, as if he couldn't stand any more.

On the bed, supported by a blushing nurse, Daisy raised a hand that trembled and pointed at Larsen. 'That's him,' she quavered. 'That was the madman's voice back there in the flat when—' She could speak no more and fell back in the nurse's arms.

Suddenly, almost startlingly, all Larsen's facial features seemed to change. Abruptly he was no longer the decent, all-American boy with his good looks and his innocent, holier-than-thou manner. Now he was a vicious, mean-faced killer, his eyes narrowed to slits, red with a burning rage. 'Don't look at me like that, you goddam limeys. I was only doing your job for you. Trying to get rid of your whores like that cunt there for you. Christ on a crutch –' his voice rose to a crescendo – 'Don't you see? I was doing you a favour. I'd—'

'Enough of that!' the Super snapped harshly. 'We've heard all we want to hear.'

The attaché opened his mouth to say something. Colonel Truscott shook his head. 'Take him outside, Major,' he commanded quietly. He's to be placed under close arrest and taken to the London stockade immediately.'

The Super opened his mouth to protest. He didn't get a chance. Suddenly Larsen lurched forward. The nurse screamed. With all his strength he slammed into the unsuspecting Super. He went down caught by surprise. Dalby tumbled over him. Mackenzie tried to grab the enraged blond giant. Larsen side-swiped him. He reeled back abruptly bleeding from his nose and mouth. Truscott lashed out with his swagger cane, crying, 'Hold it there, soldier. Hold it . . .'

But Larsen was not stopping for anyone. He sprang over the bed, with Daisy, suddenly terrified again, screaming shrilly. Next instant, Larsen had smashed through the window, showering the bed with glass. They heard him hit the ground heavily some ten feet below. A groan. A yelp of pain. Then he was up and running, while the Super still fumbled for his official police whistle and the hospital room fell into complete chaos, with the occupants shouting, yelling for help, crying contradictory orders . . .

O'Corrigan heard the crash and then the feet pounding down the street. Instinctively he knew what had happened. 'The bastard's doing a runner!' he exclaimed out loud, talking to himself in the fashion of lonely men. He didn't hesitate one moment, though he knew the police were still looking for him. At least the redcaps would be. After all, he was a military criminal on the run. He pulled off the white overall to reveal the shabby civilian suit that Paula had obtained for him on the black market. He came out of the basement and looked to left and right. No one in sight, save a water truck filling up the static water tank ready for any fires caused by the next air raid on London. Then he spotted the trail of broken glass leading off to the left and realized that must be the way the bastard Larsen had fled. Even as the main doors of the hospital were flung open and the figures in uniform came clattering down the steps, shouting and gesticulating, he was running too. The chase was on.

O'Corrigan was wary, and puzzled. He paused, watching the fugitive pass down the street, which for some reason that the Irishman couldn't understand was guarded by armed British bobbies. Were the police there looking for him, he asked himself. He dismissed the idea the next moment. British policemen were only armed for the most dire situations, not when they were looking for a squaddie who had gone on the trot. Besides, it would be the redcaps who were out looking for him. Why did they not stop the Yank? He was in uniform and he looked a mess with his torn clothes and bloodstained face, ripped by the window glass. But although they gave him a hard stare as he passed them, they made no attempt to do so.

Then he had it, for only five yards on or so, he could see the flag of the Republic of Ireland flying, with below it the brass plate bearing in Irish Gaelic and English the legend *'Embassy of the Republic of Ireland'*. It was the same with the next large house, standing in its own grounds and guarded by another armed bobby, with another uniformed man inside in a kind of sentry box. This one bore the plate reading *'Embassy of the Republic of Chile'*. Now it dawned upon him. The Ranger fugitive had not just panicked as he had sprung through the hospital window, he'd had a plan already worked out for an emergency. He'd run to one of these neutral embassies, where, once he was inside, British Law would have no jurisdiction over him. But why should one of these neutrals help a man on the run, whose photo might well be featured in the London papers on the morrow, branded as a wanted killer? What could Larsen, the vicious bastard, offer a neutral power to make up for the fact that by offering him sanctuary, they could involve themselves in a diplomatic incident with the British government? O'Corrigan frowned. At the moment he had no answer to that particular question.

'Come on Rory, lad,' he urged himself. 'Let's have a dekko where the bastard is gonna land up.' Ignoring the stares of the police as he passed them at intervals, he followed the fugitive, who was so intent on whatever he was up to that he didn't notice he was being followed.

Ahead of him, Larsen stopped at the Embassy of the Republic of Portugal. As far as O'Corrigan recalled, Portugal was supposed to be Britain's oldest ally, at least that's what they always said. But all the same, Portugal was ruled by another fascist Catholic dictator just like old de Valera over there in Dublin, his native city. Larsen couldn't expect any help from an ally of Britain, could he? Suddenly it dawned on him. Larsen was not looking for the foreign embassy of a country friendly to Britain. Totally the opposite. He was looking for one of the fascist country embassies which sided with the crooked cross of Hitler's Reich. *Great balls of frigging fire*, he exclaimed to himself, *the bastard's going to buy his freedom by selling out to the Jerries*.

A moment later that tremendous supposition was borne out as Larsen stopped outside the Embassy of the Republic of Spain and under the wary eye of the armed constable started to ring the bell at the gate which would summon the Spanish watchman. For a moment O'Corrigan steeled himself to rush the bastard and stop him by brute force. But by the time he was ready to do so, a uniformed watchman was opening the creaking gate and, with a bow, was saying,

'*A delante, señor . . . por favor . . .*' Larsen passed through and the gate closed behind him.

# Book Three: Disaster at Dieppe

'The game of espionage is too dirty for anyone but a gentleman.'

*Admiral Canaris, Head of the German* Abwehr *(Secret Service)*

# One

'What in God's name are we doing here, Mac?' Major Dalby cried above the crash of the waves against the prow of the infantry landing craft. He tugged his helmet down more tightly over his forehead with an angry gesture. 'I, for one, am too old for this sort of business.'*

Staff Sergeant Mackenzie would have laughed on any other occasion at his superior's anger. But not now. The situation was too serious. He was going into action for the very first time after being in the British Army for nearly three years.

Behind them in the landing barge, Sergeant Hawkins, the old sweat, commented, 'Won't be long now, sir. Them Jerries can't be that sleepy-headed or stupid not to know we're coming.'

Dalby nodded his head in agreement as another wave swept over the prow and lashed his face with a shower of cold water. The broad 'V' of the landing craft, plus their destroyer escorts, were heading for the cliffs which fringed the French port of Dieppe on both sides. The craft carried a whole division of Canadian troops, plus the Commando Brigade, with fifty picked Rangers attached. Yet the Germans had still not reacted.

Of course, it was not yet dawn, although the sky to

* See L. Kessler: *Murder at Colditz* for further details.

123

the east was already streaked the ugly white of the false dawn. All the same, Dalby told himself, the German radar at Dieppe should have picked up such a large force by now. Were they walking into a trap? For back in the War Office some of Dalby's senior Intelligence colleagues thought the division-sized attack was already compromised. The operation had been cancelled once and there had been too much loose talk among the Canadian assault troops and their girlfriends on the south-east coast. Still, Dalby tried to reassure himself, these girls and other hangers-on would have no means of feeding the secret information back to the Germans. For the last week the whole of the south-east coast had been monitored by the Intelligence radio-detector vans searching for illegal radio transmitters. They had found nothing.

Still Dalby was not sanguine about this first Canadian venture into Europe in World War II. Nor their own strange part in it. As he had exploded to Mackenzie when he had been first informed by the War Office of their own part in the Dieppe attack, immediately after they had been taken off the Larsen case, 'How in hell did we ever get landed with this stumer, Mac? Sent off at my age to a Commando raid. We're spy-catchers working from the comfort of an office in the War House. Cosy coal fires and cups of tea at regular intervals.'

Mackenzie had allowed himself a grin at the description, but he had said nothing; he was too eager to find out what their new mission was.

'We're supposed to be too precious, Mac, and know too much to have our tails knocked off in some derring-do foolish adventure in Occupied Europe. Can't bloody well understand it, not one bit.' He had shaken his grizzled head like a man sorely tried.

In essence they were to go on the left flank of the main

attack by the Canadians. Escorted by the Commandos and perhaps some of the new Rangers, they were to penetrate to the headquarters of the local Gestapo in Dieppe. There they were to help crack the Gestapo safe. 'What the hell do they think we are, the bloody brass hats! Crack a bloody safe, I ask you. Do they think we're bloody Bill Sykes or something?'

Now the Commandos' craft started to diverge from the main fleet, carrying the Canadians to the slaughter to come. Hawkins tightened the strap of his steel helmet, as if he were expecting trouble soon. He murmured, 'May the Lord make us truly grateful for what we are about to receive.' Next to him a big Ranger corporal said, 'You shouldn't talk like that, Sarge.'

'Like what?'

'Taking the Lord's name in vain. We want him to watch over us, ya know.'

'*Watch over us!*' Hawkins sneered. 'You wait till the shit starts flying, Yank, and then yer'll see how much watching over us the Lord'll do. He'll probably put on his dark glasses and look the other bloody way.' Then, as if he had suddenly realized the full impact of his words, the little Commando sergeant fell silent, abruptly cocooned in his own thoughts and apprehensions.

They got closer and closer to the silent port and the cliffs surrounding it. Overhead the first RAF squadrons started their dive from the sky. It was the job of the medium bombers and Spitfires to flatten the defences so that the Canadians could get their main assault weapon ashore, the new Churchill heavy tank. The tanks would lead the infantry charge up the sloping shingle beach so the Canadians could get into the port without too many initial casualties. Already the tank landing craft were beginning to lower their ramps for the tanks to scuttle off before the German guns targetted them, as they would do inevitably.

Now, just as the sun started to appear over the cliffs, a blood-red ball, flushing the sky with its light, there was a noise like a great piece of canvas being ripped apart. Smoke browned the whole of the shoreline. Cherry-red flames erupted the length of the smoke. The barrage had started. With a banshee-like howl the first great shells came hurtling down to explode in huge geysers of whirling white water around the destroyers. The Germans had been expecting them after all. The Battle for Dieppe had commenced and the Canadians would go to their deaths in their hundreds, eventually in their thousands, not knowing they had been betrayed . . .

Sweating hard, the two Intelligence men followed Hawkins' Commandos and Rangers up the fold in the cliff, which afforded them the safety of dead ground. They fought the rusty barbed wire which was everywhere among the brambles and stinging nettles. It caught and tugged at their uniforms and equipment. They cursed and pulled themselves free in an almost panic-stricken fury. For they expected the Germans at the top of the cliff to appear at any moment and begin tossing grenades down at them. The Commandos and the Rangers, trained as they were for this role, took it all in their stride, with Sergeant Hawkins hurrying them ever upwards with his 'Make it snappy, me lucky lads! Old Jerry's probably waiting on yer up there with a hot breakfast!'

But so far the 'Old Jerries' hadn't spotted these secret khaki invaders from the sea. To their surprise the two Intelligence men reached the top without a single shot being fired at them or the rest of their party. But once they breasted the top, the enemy reacted with a vengeance. Almost immediately as they started to advance, covered by their bodyguards under Hawkins, a Spandau machine gun opened up to their right. Tracer bullets, a thousand a minute, zipped flatly through the air towards them in a white lethal fury. Hastily Dalby and Mackenzie hit the ground. Not Hawkins' group of Rangers and Commandos. They surged forward. The big Ranger corporal halted in mid-stride. He heaved a grenade in the direction from which the Spandau fire was coming. 'Strike one!' he yelled, carried away by the mad unreasoning bloody fury of battle. In the same instant that it exploded in a burst of angry flame they continued their assault, firing from the hip and yelling like crazy Red Indians. For a few seconds more, the Spandau continued firing. A series of blood-curdling yells and the machine gun stuttered to a stop. Next moment the Spandau, followed by a dead machine-gunner, came hurtling out of an upstairs window and Sergeant Hawkins was calling to the two Intelligence men, 'Hurry along gentlemen . . . All aboard for the *Skylark* . . . I promise you won't get your feet wet . . .'

The little sergeant was right. Next moment they were sprinting across the coastal road and heading closer to their objective. But already they were aware that things were going wrong down on the beach to their right. One after another the new Churchill tanks were bogging down on the thick shingle located there. They slithered and skidded, trying to take the incline. Their tracks came off. Bullets howled off their sides as they stalled. Behind them the Canadian infantry, bunched together and a little out of control, went to ground and started to be mercilessly slaughtered by the German defenders, who could see every move they made. It was as if they were being served up to a cruel monster on a silver platter.

The Commando bodyguard under Sergeant Hawkins had no time for the plight of the hapless Canadian infantry.

They had been trained not to bog down, but to move fast. That way they avoided casualties. Now they moved, weaving in and out of the buildings on the cliff top, firing quick accurate bursts to left and right, clearing their path with grenades and the little 2″ mortar that they fired and fired and then moved again.

In minutes, though it seemed to Mackenzie like hours, they were doubling down the cliff road near the casino, which the Germans had taken over in 1940 when they had occupied Dieppe. Now they were firing at the upper windows of the buildings where the Germans had, in their usual fashion, placed their snipers. The Commandos knew this. Routinely they gave the upper storeys bursts of tommy-gun fire. Germans, soldiers and sailors, tumbled from the shattered windows like sacks of wet cement, dead before they slammed into the cobbled *pavé* below.

Mackenzie, head ducked in his collar, as if that might protect him as the slugs howled off the buildings all around, could see the Canadians down below were taking an awful beating. Right from the waterline to the edge of the shingle shore, there were neat lines of their dead, shot as if by a firing squad. Most of them, it was clear, had died before they could even fire their own weapons. Now the assault infantry were split into little groups, some disorganized, wondering whether to go backwards or forwards. Others under the command of brave and gallant young subalterns and NCOs tried to push on with the desperate courage of men who knew they were going to die, but were going to show something of worth for their supreme sacrifice. But the great majority of the survivors, many wounded, had crawled behind the cover of the wrecked, smouldering Churchills and simply let events take their course.

Still the Commandos and their US trainees advanced. It was almost as if they were on an exercise back in the UK.

Everything they did was purposeful and well thought out in advance. Hawkins didn't even have to give many orders. The men did what they had to do instinctively without having to be told . . . Once it seemed they might be stopped by two German marines operating a small mortar from the back garden of one of the cliff-top houses. They weren't. Without Hawkins ordering them to do anything, four of the leading Commandos produced smoke grenades. As one they pitched them. In an instant the German marines were blinded by thick white pungent smoke. The attackers didn't give them a chance to run for it. Three other Commandos sprinted forward. One of them carried a small round pack on his shoulders. For a moment a petrified Mackenzie was puzzled by the object. Not for long.

The one with the pack stumbled to a halt, while his bodyguards snapped off quick, aimed shots to left and right. Legs spread like some western gunslinger in a Hollywood epic, he pressed the trigger of his terrible weapon. A sound like some great primeval monster drawing a fiery breath. Angry snarling blue and red flame spurted from its nozzle. It slapped the building audibly, curled round it, blackening everything in its path, and struck the smoke-blinded mortar crew.

Screaming frantically, the bodies aflame in an instant, trying to put out the flames with hands that were alight themselves and were rapidly turning into charred shrivelled claws, they staggered a few paces into the street. Next moment they collapsed in pools of burning oil-mix, transformed into shrunken charred pygmies before Mackenzie's horrified gaze. Behind him the big Ranger corporal choked, as if he might start vomiting at any moment, and said hoarsely, 'Is it possible?'

'Yer,' Hawkins butted in, his old sweat's face hard and taut and glistening. 'It frigging . . . well is.' He coughed thickly with the smoke. 'That's war.' He indicated the two charred German marines, twitching in their death throes, skeletal black claws held upright, as if appealing to a God who was looking the other way. 'Come on now, don't frig about. There's our objective o'er there.' He indicated the Gestapo building. 'Gildy now, lads!'

A couple of hundred miles away, O'Corrigan sweated in his thick serge suit, as he waited in the warm August sunshine, together with Paula. She had insisted on coming with him this time, saying, 'A bloke with a woman, especially one like me who seems posh, looks less suspicious, Rory.' And he had been forced to agree. For days now he had been observing the Spanish legation and he reasoned that sooner or later one of the Spanish security guards or perhaps even the bored policemen might notice his presence there every day and start asking awkward questions.

Now they watched the tall nineteenth-century house, set well back from the street, intently, noting the usual comings and goings, but, as O'Corrigan had found out already, with no sign of Larsen. All the same he was sure that the big Ranger was still in the neutral embassy. Twice he had observed the place late at night when he thought the Spaniards might have attempted to smuggle out the wanted man. But once more he had drawn a blank.

'You know, Paula, we can guess the Spaniards are pumping him –' he meant Larsen – 'for anything he can pass on to the Jerries. But why are they keeping him so long? What could a bastard and pervert like Larsen know of great importance? Besides, Paula, they must have some idea of the kind of swine they're harbouring. I mean, they won't need a crystal ball to work out who he is – from what has appeared in the newspapers so far.' He frowned with bewilderment.

'Perhaps this here Larsen knows more than you think,

Rory?' she suggested. 'Look out, a rozzer!' she hissed urgently.

'Christ!' O'Corrigan cursed. He wasn't afraid, but he didn't want to be apprehended yet until he found Larsen and squeezed the truth about the grenade incident from the big blond bastard.

'Leave it to me,' she muttered hastily, as the solid middle-aged policeman approached. Hastily she snuggled closer to a sweating O'Corrigan and said in pure Cockney, 'So this here Yank and the little Cockney tart was standing at the street corner when the wind blew up the tart's skirt and, as she was on business and wasn't wearing no knickers, you could see everything – what she had for breakfast like. And the Yank said, "'Airy, ain't it?" and she sez, cheeky-like, "What did yer expect, Yank – *feavvers!*"'

Rory forced a laugh and the constable, hearing the punchline, said, 'Now, now, miss, we don't want none o' that kind of dirty talk around here. Posh folk live here, yer know.' But there was a twinkle in his eyes as he plodded on in the ponderous manner of the police, muttering to himself, 'What der yer expect, Yank – *feathers!*'

O'Corrigan breathed a sigh of relief. 'For half a mo I thought he was going to try to nick us for loitering with intent. Some trumped-up charge.'

She squeezed him softly. 'Daft bugger. Not when you're with me, dearie,' she said winningly. 'Anyone looking at yours truly can tell I'm as honest as the day's long.'

'If you say so,' the Irishman answered and his face grew sombre once more. 'You see, Paula. I want to nail the bastard, as I've said, because he's done something very wrong. I want to clear myself naturally, too. But above all I want to get back into the war again. I want to go overseas. The air of the front is cleaner than all this.' He made a vague gesture that encompassed the embassies, but might well have done the whole of Britain, too.

She looked anxious. 'Don't talk like that, Rory. You've done yer bit. You've bin wounded twice and you won that good gong. Even got it from that poor stuttering sod, the King.'

O'Corrigan nodded, his mind already elsewhere, back to that cleaner air of the front, where you knew who your friends were and there was none of this bloody backbiting and career-building of the home front. He wanted war, violent action and, in the end, death itself. But he didn't dare tell Paula that. She loved him in her fashion. Instead he said, 'If we could only tempt the bugger out and nab him. He won't get away from me a second time, I can tell you that, Paula.'

For what seemed a long while they stood there in the shade, saying nothing, listening to the lazy hum of the bees in the hollyhocks in the garden behind them. Then the noise of an old taxi, backfiring at intervals and filling the air suddenly with the stink of burning oil, roused them from their self-induced lethargy.

They turned to watch it approach, half aware that something was afoot. It was. The taxi halted. An obvious Spaniard with dark, sleeked-back hair, carrying the diplomat's customary rolled umbrella and bowler, clad in a kind of morning suit in spite of the warmth of the day, opened the rear door. He indicated something to the cab driver, paid him and then held out his hand to a rather fat blonde in ATS uniform, which fitted her very badly. Over the road, the guard started to open the big iron gate of the Spanish Embassy after the dark-haired man had ordered, '*Abierto – pronto!*' The unlikely pair were about to enter the Embassy.

Next to O'Corrigan Paula gave a little gasp. 'Cor, stone the crows, what's she doing in ATS togs?'

'Who?'

'Madame over yonder. Old Juicy Lucy. Christ, she must be fifty if she's a day. Why, she's bin on the game so long that they've had to fit her out with a cunt made o' leather.'

It was then that O'Corrigan had his daring idea.

# Two

'Here we are, gents,' Sergeant Hawkins said expansively, ignoring the stream of tracer flying over the Commandos' heads, 'it's all yours. The Jerries have done a bunk . . . well, some of them have.' He indicated the dead German sprawled out in the hallway in the extravagant pose of those done violently to death. 'It's all yours.' Without waiting for the two Intelligence officers to react to his invitation, Sergeant Hawkins started rapping out orders to his little bunch of Commandos and Rangers. 'All right, Jenkins, you up on the roof with the Bren gun. You, Slack-arse round the back with your Sten. If they come, don't open fire. Just give us the wire. You, Yank, take the rear window. Keep a weather eye on what's going on down there on the beach.'

Mackenzie didn't need to look in that direction. He could tell by the sound of the firing, now predominantly German, with little response from the stalled Canadians, that things were going badly down there. The sooner they had completed their task here at the Gestapo HQ and were on their way back to the boats, the better. Dieppe was obviously turning into a bloody nightmare for the attackers.

Dalby seemed to read his mind. He drew his .38 and snapped, 'Come on, Mac. We can't risk these men much longer. Sergeant Hawkins. You got the necessary?'

'Yessir,' the little old sweat responded promptly. 'Like the boy scouts, we're always prepared.'

They wasted no more time. They entered the head-quarters, which smelt of age, garlic and strong French cigarettes – and fear, abject fear. For this had been a place of torture, and Mackenzie, who wasn't really an imaginative young man, could feel the terror the building gave off.

There was paper strewn everywhere. Here and there little fires flickered, with ash wafting down the corridor, as if the flown Gestapo torturers had tried to burn secret documents before they had run for it. Hanging from the back of an overturned chair there was a pair of sheer black silk knickers. Why, Mackenzie couldn't fathom.

They penetrated deeper into the house of torture. Now the sound of the battle outside became muted. On the walls were pictures of the Nazi *Prominenz* – Gestapo Müller, Reichsführer SS Himmler, the Führer. But they had no eyes for them. They had to get in and out – *fast*. Time was running out.

They passed a large study. Its door hung at an angle by a single hinge. It had been shattered by the bomb which had exploded outside during the RAF attack. On the chaise longue inside, a half-naked woman rested, as if she were sleeping gently. But her naked breasts, which lolled to one side, didn't move. Dalby said in a matter-of-fact tone, 'She's dead.' He shrugged. 'A patriot or a common whore? Who knows. Doesn't matter now.'

'Sir.' Mackenzie broke into Dalby's little reverie. 'Behind that picture over the fireplace.' He indicated a stylized portrait of the heroic Waffen SS fighting in the snows of Russia, which had been shredded by shrapnel and now was hanging at an angle. 'The safe, sir.'

Dalby moved smartly. 'Sergeant Hawkins. You ready?'

135

Hawkins took his eyes off the large breasts with their great dun-coloured nipples, which would never be fondled and excited again. 'In a brace of shakes, sir.' He pulled a string of what looked like kid's plasticine out of his battledress blouse, where he had kept it so that it remained soft and malleable. The substance gave off a strong odour of almonds. 'Plastic explosive, sir,' he explained. 'Latest thing.' Without another word, he stuck a time pencil into the new form of explosive, placed it around the safe's combination lock and pulled the time pencil's string to arm it. 'Stand back, gents. We've got one minute exactly.'

Hurriedly they ducked behind the big easy chairs, the ashtrays strapped across their arms, filled with the cigar butts of the hurriedly departed Gestapo torturers. '*One . . . two . . . three*,' Hawkins counted off and opened his mouth very wide so that the blast wouldn't shatter his eardrums. The plastic explosive detonated. A cloud of pungent smoke, metal tore. The door of the safe fell open to reveal – *nothing!*

For a moment Mackenzie and Dalby froze. They stared at each other in blank amazement. Outside the battle raged furiously. They didn't seem to hear it; they were too shocked. Finally Dalby found his voice. 'We've been sent here on a wild goose chase,' he said to no one in particular. 'There are no papers . . . Perhaps never were any . . .'

'Sir,' Sergeant Hawkins cut in sharply. At the rear window the American Ranger was firing short, sharp bursts with his tommy gun at someone further down the street and Hawkins knew what that meant. The Germans were rallying on the cliff top and coming their way. 'For Chrissakes, let's get out o' here before it's too late.'

Still bewildered, but realizing the danger, Major Dalby let himself be guided outside as the mixed group of

British and American special forces started to fall back. But Hawkins, old hand that he was, was not taking the same route which they had used to approach the Gestapo HQ. 'They'll have snipers at every upstairs window,' he shouted over the angry snap-and-crack of the small arms fight. 'Follow me this way.'

They swung themselves over the side of the cliff. Down below a bunch of the Commandos in stocking caps were holding a small bridgehead. Further up the beach where the Canadians had landed, the massacre continued. Now and again Mackenzie risked a glance in that direction as he descended the steep cliff, with Dalby being aided by Hawkins to his front. There were heaps of Canadian dead piled like gory logs everywhere. Suddenly he was overwhelmed by a tremendous sense of helplessness as a young bareheaded Canadian, obviously badly wounded and crawling on all fours, shouted at the dead in a crazy fashion, 'Christ, boys, we've gotta beat 'em . . . We've just gotta.' A moment later a sniper's bullet took him at the back of the head. His skull shattered in a gory welter of blood and he dropped face forward in the sand and shingle.

Dalby saw the death too. The old major, who had seen death often enough in the trenches of the First War cried harshly, 'Come, Mac, stop looking like a fart in a trance.' Dalby wasn't usually coarse. But Mackenzie knew the reason why he was now; he wanted him, and anyone else for that matter, not to succumb to despair. They had to keep moving, whatever happened.

Sergeant Hawkins got hit first. 'Bugger it!' he moaned and then, letting go of his hold, went tumbling and slithering down the rest of the cliff to the sand. 'Hell,' Mackenzie cried. 'Hawkins . . .'

'All right, sir,' the little old sweat called weakly. 'They ain't gonna get Mrs Hawkins' handsome son that—' He broke off with another groan and clutched his skinny chest, his fingers pressed tightly together. Bright red blood started to seep through immediately.

Mackenzie knew he ought to do something. He took a chance. Letting go of his hold, he dropped heavily to the sand. For a moment he was winded. Then keeping low, as tracer whizzed back and forth in a lethal morse and out at sea the destroyers began bombarding the shore, he crawled to where Hawkins writhed in the sand. 'How are you?' he gasped foolishly.

'All right, as long as I don't laugh,' Hawkins said, his face screwed up with the agony of the wound, which had torn the front of his chest apart. Through the gory mess, Mackenzie could see the lungs pulsating, a great grey mass. He realized that under present conditions, the old sweat wasn't going to survive. Still he said,

'Soon have you on board one of the landing craft. You'll be right as rain, once we get you back to Blighty.'

Weakly Hawkins shook his head. He bit his bottom lip till the blood came, then forced himself to speak, his head lolling from one side to the other, as if he were racked by almost unbearable pain. 'No Blighty for me, Mac . . . Mr O'Corrigan, see he's done right by.'

'Don't worry—'

Hawkins cut him short. 'I helped him, Mac . . . get away . . .' He was uttering the words in short agonized gasps. 'Big Smoke . . . He has a tart there . . . she's putting him up . . .'

A salvo of 4.5" naval guns thundered overhead like a midnight express roaring through a deserted provincial station. Mackenzie strained to hear the rest of the dying NCO's words.

'Tart with a snake . . . dancer . . .' the words trailed away to nothing. Hawkins' head fell to one side. Blood trickled out of the side of his mouth. Hastily Mackenzie felt for his pulse. Nothing. The old sweat was dead. For a moment he didn't know what to do. He simply knelt there, oblivious to the bullets striking the sand in vicious little flurries all around him. Then the rest of them were dropping beside him in the sand, with the Germans suddenly appearing on the cliff top looking for 'Tommies' to kill. They knew they had the Anglo-Americans on the run and for a little while the latter were sitting ducks as they waited for the landing barge to take them off. Soon the stick grenades would come hurtling down on them. The Commandos knew that. So did Major Dalby. Winded and shaky as he was from the climb down the cliff, he ordered, 'All right, pull back to the barge . . . Fire at will.' As if to emphasize his order, he pulled out his revolver again and, with a hand that trembled badly, he fired up at the Germans. Above them a German Marine screamed. He clawed the air, as if he were attempting to climb the rungs of an invisible ladder. Next moment, he pitched face forward over the edge of the cliff, dead before he hit the sand below.

Now they started to retreat, pausing every few seconds to fire at the Germans above them. Stick grenades were falling on all sides. Sand flew upwards in great gouts. Shrapnel, red-hot and cruelly jagged, cut the air frighteningly. Men were hit. They yelped with pain, but staggered on. Up at the bows a tousled sailor – he looked no more than fourteen – had set up a Lewis gun. With a fag out of the side of his mouth, he was firing controlled bursts at the Germans, a happy grin on his face. 'Good for you, sailor!' Major Dalby yelled encouragingly. 'Keep up the good—' His words died as the grenade exploded only feet away. For a moment he was engulfed in white smoke. Next he was falling to the scuffed body-littered sand, his face an ashen white, blood spurting from a badly shattered leg in a bright red arc.

Mackenzie rushed to him. Someone shouted urgently. 'No stopping for casualties . . . that's an order.' Mackenzie wasn't listening. He knelt at Dalby's side. The leg was split open right to the thigh. Through the blackened, ripped trouser leg, he could see the shattered bone gleaming like polished white ivory against the red gore. Mackenzie remembered his first aid. He grasped the upper part of the major's leg and pressed hard. The bleeding seemed to diminish for a minute, but only for a minute. As soon as he let go, the great gaping wound started to pump blood once again. The American corporal peered over his shoulder. 'No use, Sarge,' he commented. 'He needs proper medical attention. He'll croak before we can get him back to England.'

Mackenzie was in a quandary. He knew he couldn't risk these brave men's lives by waiting here for some sort of medic to turn up; at the same time he just couldn't abandon Major Dalby. 'But they might shoot the major . . .' he objected.

'Ner,' a little Commando said, blood pouring down the side of his head from a nasty scalp wound. 'The Jerries don't shoot wounded, even when they're Commandos. They'll look after him. OK, Staff. Come on, we'd better bugger off before they start coming down the cliff.'

'Do as they say, Mac,' Dalby said weakly from the sand, his eyelids flickering open for a moment. He tried to force a smile of encouragement, but failed miserably. 'I've had it . . . Cut off home.'

'But sir—'

'No buts,' Dalby cut him short. 'You're needed back there . . . Ask why we got involved in this balls-up . . .'

140

His eyeballs started to roll upwards and Mackenzie could see that he was about to lapse into unconsciousness once again.

'Needed, sir?'

'Yes, this Gestapo business . . .'*

'You men,' the harsh metallic tone of a loudspeaker from the barge cut in, even above the chatter of the old-fashioned Lewis. 'Get aboard. We're sailing.'

'At the double, lads,' someone cried.

The Commandos needed no urging. They started to back off once more, firing from the hip as they did so. Germans began pitching over the side of the cliff, but others had used the cover of a gully to come in from the flank. Now they were not more than fifty or so yards away. Mackenzie looked at them and then down at Dalby. His mind racing wildly, he wondered whether he should stay behind with Dalby. But what would that achieve? First the major would go into hospital. When he recovered, if he did, he'd be sent into an officers' POW camp. He, Mackenzie, would be dispatched to a Stalag reserved for other ranks. They'd never see each other again till the end of the war anyway.

Mackenzie made his decision, wondering what the future held for his desperately wounded boss. Weakly Dalby reached out and touched Mackenzie's hand. Then his head lolled to one side and he was unconscious once more and on the barge the ratings were gunning their engines impatiently as the victorious Germans got closer and closer. Obediently Mackenzie followed the rest, defeated and deflated as the survivors all were. As the barge, its screws churning crazily, started to move out into the deeper water, the

* See Leo Kessler: *Murder at Colditz* (Severn House) for further details.

sweating Germans on the beach removed their helmets and some of them actually waved. They didn't fire any more. It was as if they did not find the 'Tommies' worthy of having another bullet wasted on them . . .

# Three

The Spanish watchman mopped his brow and breathed out hard, '*Hombre!*' he swore. '*El Americano es totalmente loco – fuerte, también.*' He breathed on his smarting bruised knuckles like a boxer might do after a hard contest in the ring.

Don Alfredo de Rosas y Figueres was not impressed. What these peasants got up to was really not his concern. Still, he was curious enough to ask, 'What did he do to the woman this time?'

'Nearly strangled her, *señor*,' the watchman answered. 'At the beginning it was all *amor y pesatas*. Then when he didn't get from her –' he made an explicit sexual gesture with his forefinger and thumb formed into a circle and the forefinger of his other hand thrusting in and out of the circle – 'you know.'

The sleek-haired diplomat nodded and the strong-looking watchman continued with, 'Then he went crazy. She was cursed as a godless whore, who should die for her sins. If me and Miguel hadn't got hold of him in time, he'd have strangled the poor woman to death.'

The diplomat shrugged carelessly. 'She's only a common whore.'

'*Puta o no puta*, she is a woman,' the man chided him.

'Remember your place,' the diplomat snapped acidly.

'*Lo siento.*'

For a moment the diplomat stared at the yellowing portrait of Philip II on the wall of the embassy's great hall and wondered why the soldier-emperor hadn't dealt with the English once and for all back in the sixteenth century. Then he dismissed the thought and said, 'Make sure he had no access to knives or anything sharp.'

'*Y hecho*,' the other man replied.

'*Bueno*. See he gets as much as he wants to drink and if necessary give him a drug. Tell him, if he asks, we have hired another whore for him for the weekend.'

The watchman frowned. 'Must he have one?'

'Mind your business,' the diplomat said icily. 'Leave the thinking to your betters. Now get about your work.'

The watchman gave a slight bow and turned, raging inwardly. These damned Catalans, he told himself, were the arse of a mule. General Franco should have killed off every last one back in '39 when he had captured the damned Red province.

Alone, the diplomat wondered at the '*Americano*'. He might be an unbeliever, a follower of that damned Martin Luther, an arch enemy of the Holy Catholic Church, yet he was devout in his strange way. But despite his obvious piety, that American was the most vicious man he had ever met, and he had met many vicious men during the recent fighting in Spain. How could the human brain understand such a combination?

After all, standing there alone in the gloomy hall which smelt of furniture polish and ancient furniture, brought from one of the looted *Paradores* to fill it, Don Alfredo decided he couldn't. It would be better to work out the details of getting rid of the American as soon as possible before these cunning aristocratic English dandies of the British Foreign Office began making representations to Madrid in order to get their hands on the fugitive, once they had discovered he was hiding in the Spanish legation.

The valet caught him by surprise. He came in almost noiselessly. Indeed, he had to clear his throat in the manner of servants before the diplomat became aware of his presence. '*Señor*,' he said in that modulated quiet tone of the good servant.

He turned, surprised.

'*Oigo?*' he answered.

'*Las noticias*,' the servant replied. '*De Alemania . . . Creo . . . muy importante.*'

The diplomat was awake immediately. He nodded. Together the two of them, the valet holding out his white-gloved hand like a head waiter leading in a client who tipped well, went into the radio room, where the operator was waiting for him. Already he had loosened his earphones, in case the diplomat wanted them.

Swiftly he grabbed them and held them close to his ears. He understood German, but he had to listen carefully in order not to miss anything. But the news had not really started. Instead there was the usual bombastic blare of military music which heralded a victory, followed by the harsh-voiced speaker announcing, '*Das Oberkommando der deutschen Wehrmacht gibt bekannt.*' Then it followed. 'The Greater German Army informs us that our brave German Armed Forces have achieved yet another victory over the decadent plutocratic Jewish Anglo-American troops. Yesterday the German *Wehrmacht* repelled an attempted enemy invasion of the continental mainland. It was a decisive victory with a whole Canadian division, six thousand men strong, virtually wiped out.'

There was a pause, filled out with Hitler's favourite military march, the 'Badenweiler'. Then the speaker's intense, over-excited voice came back. He cried, 'Now,

General Field Marshal von Rundstedt has this to say to you from his headquarters in France. Over to Paris.'

Another slight pause. A thin, rather quavering voice came on to say, '*Meine Damen und Herren*, I am pleased to say confidently that we will not be seeing the English on this side of the Channel for the rest of this war. Our brave German soldiers have seen to that yesterday at Dieppe. You may take my word for it as German Field Marshal that the English are finished in Europe . . .'

The weak, cognac-heavy voice vanished, to be replaced by more bombastic brassy martial music.

The diplomat nodded to the white-gloved valet. Instantly he turned off the radio. The diplomat said, 'Bring me some champagne – *French*. It is an occasion to be celebrated.'

'*Si señor.*'

The valet vanished, silent in his rubber-soled shoes. The diplomat relaxed a little in the hard wooden seventeenth-century chair. It had all worked out well, he told himself. Admiral Canaris, his master, who supplied him with the drugs without which he couldn't live, would be pleased. As for the ambassador, he would be too. They had done what they could for the Germans. Now it would be time to return to normal embassy business. General Franco would be happy too. This kind of success at Dieppe would mean the *Caudillo* would be able to press even more to ensure that Gibraltar was returned to Spanish hands after nearly three hundred years of cruel English occupation.

He pondered the problem of the mad American in the basement of the embassy once more. He and the others who were in on the plot had already considered several ways of getting him out of the damned little island before he became a diplomatic liability. Someone had suggested – as a joke – that they should 'get rid of him in the diplomatic pouch'.

The others had laughed at that. He hadn't. His mind had concentrated on that 'get rid of him', the phrase that the First Secretary had used. It would be much easier to kill the American. There were enough servants in the embassy who had killed more than once during the Civil War; indeed, a few of them gloried in their exploits, going on at length about how they had shot the reds in Barcelona or the foreigners they had taken prisoner when they had fought the International Brigade on the Ebro. But he knew the others, in particular the First Secretary, wouldn't accept that solution. Like most diplomats who created wars they were lily-livered when it came to the actual killing.

So they had talked over their champagne of the other means of smuggling the American out of England. By air was out of the question. There were naturally no direct flights to Madrid; planes to the Spanish capital would have to fly over German-occupied territory and the English couldn't do that. There were weekly flights by flying boat from Southampton to Lisbon in Portugal. But he had found out that passengers on those flights were checked and re-checked by English security. In the end he, at least, had come to the conclusion that the only way was to smuggle the American on a neutral Irish ship to Southern Ireland. The diplomat knew there were enough Irishmen who hated the English and with the help of a handful of sovereigns would be only too willing to smuggle another 'patriot' out of the clutches of the English oppressors.

The diplomat paused for a moment. He looked to left and right. No one. On impulse he took the silver tube out of his waistcoat pocket, plus the screw of paper that contained what he called his 'lifesaver'. He had intended to use a pinch on the end of his penis that night when he visited his mistress in Mayfair; he found the drug prolonged his pleasure. Now, however, he needed its mental stimulation.

147

He had to think this thing with the damned American through and come up with a final solution. The drug would help, he knew; it always did.

Carefully he unfolded the paper. He shook it gently so that every grain of the precious drug was freed for inhaling. Now he placed the silver tube up his right nostril, pressed the other one closed, and sniffed hard. He grunted with pleasure, imagining that the coke was already having an effect. Then he did the same with the other nostril until all the white powder had vanished from the paper; and as it did, already feeling that familiar sensation, the only one that made life worth living, he told himself the American was becoming too much of a problem. Perhaps there were other ways of dealing with him . . .

In the basement, locked in his bedroom once more, Larsen lay naked on the bed, holding his flaccid penis. His mood was a mixture of pleasant relief and a latent anger. He didn't like the dagoes. They were papist for one thing – they were always crossing themselves and they had a tame priest even, who smelt of incense and brandy. They didn't trust him either, although he had brought the vital news about Dieppe. That surely must have gotten the dagoes well in with the Kraut, Hitler. All the same he knew they'd get rid of him as soon as they could. Now he had nothing more to offer them. He guessed he was an embarrassment to them, the lousy Catholics. Christ, sometimes he thought they were worse than the Mexes – and there was nothing worser than the Mexicans.

Idly he toyed with his penis. But it remained stubbornly soft. So he let his mind drift to the early hours of that morning, just before the whore they had smuggled in for him was about to depart in the taxi waiting outside for her. She had just slipped on her drawers when on impulse he had ripped down the front and gazed lecherously at her thick patch of dark pubic hair, through which her labia peeped a delicate pink. 'Je–sus,' he had drooled, licking his thick sensuous lips, 'what a lovely snatch. I think I could do another slice of that cookie, momma.'

She had pushed his hand away with a grumpy, 'Not on yer nelly, Yank. You've had yer bellyful o' pie for this day. Anyhow my taxi's waiting outside.'

'Screw the taxi,' he had snarled. 'Come on, momma, give out.' He had grabbed her hard and pulled her to him, the muscles rippling across his shoulders cruelly. He felt himself grow hard again. He tightened his grip, his big fingers digging into the soft flesh of her bottom. Suddenly the whore had heaved with fear like a trapped animal. 'Please,' she whimpered, 'don't hurt me . . . Just let me go . . . I ain't done yer no harm, Yank, have I?'

He had grinned at her frightened coarse face. 'Ner,' he answered through gritted teeth, feeling that old urge come over him. 'You ain't done me no harm.' Deliberately he imitated her cockney whine. 'It's me who's gonna do *you* some harm, baby.' He freed one hand and pushed it between her legs, forcing them apart. He felt her vulva and exclaimed, 'Biggest muff I've seen for a long time, sister. But it's dry and tight as a drum, you bitch. Don't worry, I'll fix you.' He let go of her leg and with a grunt, feeling his heart pounding frantically with ever-increasing excitement, reached beneath the bed where he had concealed it. His sweaty hand closed on its hard steel coolness. God, he was coming already!

She freed her head from where he had pulled it tight to his chest and stared up at his sweat-glazed, contorted face, his eyes seeming to be about to pop out of his head. 'What yer gonna do?' she began. Then she saw the knife and cried in a little trembling voice, 'Oh, gawd, what's that thing for?'

He licked his lips, which had become very dry abruptly. 'What do you think, stupid?'

The whore had seen men like this before. Mostly they had been the impotent ones, who couldn't get their pecker up and took it out on women by beating them up. Not this one. He was too damned virile. He needed no substitute for a 'John Thomas' that wouldn't perform. But he was going to hurt her, the whore knew that. It was then in acute desperation that she had managed to scream and that goddam dago fag, who minced and smelled of expensive cologne, had burst into the bedroom. His eyes had taken in the scene immediately. '*Bastante!*' he had cried. '*Bastante para hoy!*' Then in English, 'That's enough of that, Larsen. Stop it!'

Still keeping his tight grip on the whore, but managing to hide the knife and let it fall silently to the carpeted floor, he had sneered, 'Don't tell me *you're* going to make me stop, Pancho!'

The diplomat hadn't hesitated. As if by magic a small silver pistol had appeared in his hand and its muzzle was pointing right at Larsen's head. 'I'll blow your damned head off – just like that. I can do anything here. We have no police. You're a dead man, Larsen, if you don't let go of the woman immediately.'

Larsen could see the dago wasn't joking. He pinched the whore's nipple cruelly and she cried out in pain, but he let go all the same and she fled to the Spaniard sobbing as if her heart were broken. For a moment the Spaniard had looked at him very hard, then when it seemed he was sure that the naked American giant wasn't going to spring from the bed and attack him, he lowered the pistol. 'Get dressed now,' he ordered the whore.

'Don't leave me, sir,' she quavered.

'I won't.'

Hastily she pulled on her outer clothing, not even bother-
ing to look in her handbag to check if the money he
had been allowed to give her was still there; she was
too afraid.

For what seemed a long time the two men continued
to stare at each other in a heavy silence, both of them
wrapped in a cocoon of their own thoughts, and they
weren't pleasant. Then, outside, the taxi sounded its horn
and they were gone, leaving Larsen, his heart full of hatred
for the woman, the dago, the whole damn world.

Now Larsen was plagued by a sense of unease. Naturally
at first the dagoes had welcomed him with open arms when
he had hinted what he knew. They'd contacted Berlin
straightaway after talking with Madrid. Berlin had apparently been ecstatic. The diplomat, who was the Spanish
Embassy's Intelligence man, had said that Berlin had
promised him a safe haven, a new passport and money
and the freedom to pick his country of refuge himself. He
could go anywhere from Switzerland to South America to
start a new life. Christ on a Crutch, the dagoes had been
eating out of his hand and he could have as many whores
as he could handle.

That had been at the beginning. Now he had betrayed the
secret of Dieppe to them, he had a feeling that the mood in
the Spanish Embassy was changing. He could offer them
and their Kraut friends little more and that last threat of
the fag dago had convinced him they might well think it
better to get rid of him by pushing him down a hole into
the Thames. Why bother to send him to Berlin?

Larsen forgot about his limp organ. He rose from the bed.
Silently he padded to the door. It was locked, of course,
he knew. Still, he tested it, turning the handle carefully in
case his watchman was outside. The handle seemed stiff.
Perhaps, he told himself, they had put another lock on since

he had come to the embassy. All the same he had his knife. Perhaps he could use it to open the lock? The Commandos had trained him and his fellow Rangers to do such things. He abandoned the lock and its problems for a moment.

He crossed to the large window. The blackout curtains were still drawn. Carefully he parted the left one and, kneeling low so that he was not exposed to any watcher, he peered out. The street was getting light now. At the far end there was the usual milk float drawn by a bow-headed, skinny-ribbed nag that looked as if it was on its last legs. Beyond, a policeman, armed, stood in the shadows watching the embassy. Otherwise there were no Spanish watchmen in sight. That was a good sign. Typical dago. They always goofed off whenever they thought it safe. Gingerly, very gingerly, not wanting to make any noise, he tried the window. As he had half expected, it was fastened. But not so securely. The bolt rattled slightly. It sounded to Larsen as if the wood halfway up might have warped and the screws which held the bolt in place could be loose.

Hurriedly he padded to where he had hidden the knife. He had stolen it from his breakfast tray two days before and had assiduously sharpened its blade on the rough stone of the big open fireplace. Now the blade was razor sharp and honed to a point like a screwdriver. He placed the end in the first of the screws. It turned easily. The others did the same. Five or ten minutes later he had freed the bolt and taking his time, holding his breath instinctively, lifted the bottom half of the window until it could go no further. He beamed. The window was the way out. He had an escape route.

Thoughtfully he returned to bed and lay down, his hand reaching down for his penis. He squeezed it a couple of times. It started to grow hard. That was a good sign. He was in form again and he had a plan. All he needed now was a woman. But not just for sex. She was going to be part of his escape plan and he knew that if he kicked up enough fuss the dago faggot would supply him with one just to keep him quiet. Pleased with himself he started to masturbate.

# Four

It was two weeks now since the terrible debacle at Dieppe. Mackenzie had landed at Newhaven with the rest of the survivors, many of them wounded, to be posed in front of the newsreel cameras and the press photographers and told to smile and 'remember you're British', to which one grumpy Commando, bloody bandage wound around his head, growled, 'Ay, but them buggers over there in France didn't seem to know that, mate.'

But with the propaganda photos, the pressmen encouraging those who posed with cries of 'Are we downhearted, mates?' and the like, Mackenzie, as filthy and worn as he was, had found himself hurried to a Humber staff car and whisked off to London in grand style. In the back of the big staff car, there had even been a wicker hamper containing ham sandwiches, pork pies – a rare delicacy – a thermos of hot tea and half a bottle of Haig whisky. That half bottle of scotch made Mackenzie start to worry. Other ranks didn't often receive the honour of a staff car, complete with pretty ATS chauffeur and half a bottle of whisky.

The young staff sergeant's concern grew even more when at the War Office he was ushered into the presence of no less a person than the 'Hangman's Dilemma', Brigadier Kenneth Strong, Britain's most senior Intelligence officer: smart and multilingual and possessing virtually no chin so that his subordinates quipped no hangman could keep the noose in place if it ever came to Strong being hanged; hence his nickname.

In his thick Scots accent, the Hangman's Dilemma got down to business at once. He rose – surprisingly for a brigadier – and shook Mackenzie's hand, saying, 'Good show, Mackenzie. Sorry to hear about your chief. I've got my feelers out in Berlin. We'll soon find out what happened to Major Dalby. Now sit down and I'll ring for some tea.'

Mackenzie was totally bemused by the brigadier's behaviour and especially the way Strong had remarked so casually that he'd soon have knowledge of what had happened to Dalby – *from Berlin!* It was almost as if the Hangman's Dilemma popped over to the enemy capital every week or so for a chat with his cronies from his days as the pre-war British military attaché in Berlin.

Tea was served on a silver platter and from a silver Queen Anne teapot and it was real 'Sar'nt-Major's char', made with creamy tinned milk, totally unlike the sugarless, bitter liquid offered normally to 'other ranks'. There were even chocolate finger biscuits of a kind that an overwhelmed Mackenzie had not seen since before the war, when as a PhD student he wouldn't have been able to afford them anyway.

Strong gave him his toothy smile and began with, 'Congratulations, Mackenzie.'

'Congratulations, sir?'

'Yes, we've put you in for a commission. 'Bout time you became an officer and a gentleman.' He beamed at the surprised young man. 'You'll be gazetted to the Intelligence Corps at the end of August. You deserve it for all the good work you've put in since '39.'

'Thank you, sir . . . very kind of you, sir,' Mackenzie heard himself saying from far away as if in a dream.

Strong's face became stern now and he turned very businesslike. 'Now we're going to forget this sorry business with Major Dalby for the time being . . . the fiasco with the Gestapo HQ and the rest of it. You understand?' It wasn't a question; it was an order, Mackenzie realized. He answered promptly, 'Yessir!' though he would dearly have loved to have known more of that particular mystery, which had cost Major Dalby his freedom at Dieppe.

'What concerns us – *you* – now is the question of who betrayed the Dieppe op to the Hun. I mean, the mission was compromised several times after the first plan was called off when the assault troops were already in their boats. But since that time the plan had been changed considerably. So we can conclude that the person or persons who betrayed the plan to the Germans was conversant with the second plan. That limits our field of suspects to senior Canadian and British officers and, in particular, to the Commando-Ranger group, even down to the other-rank level.'

Mackenzie heard himself agreeing with the Hangman's Dilemma.

'Well, as you know Mackenzie, there are two likely candidates in that force of British and American special troops who could have betrayed the plan – somehow or other – to the Huns: Ranger Larsen, the American, and this O'Corrigan, who's on the run.' He paused, his dark eyes thoughtful, and Mackenzie told himself that although Strong looked the typical chinless wonder one often found on the staff, this man was clever, very clever. Strong's next words proved it. 'Although I have absolutely no evidence that O'Corrigan didn't blab to the Germans – why shouldn't he, after all, he had been given a very rough and unfair deal at that court martial – I don't think he did. His whole record shows him to be a very loyal soldier, who, although he came from Southern Ireland, has fought bravely and at some cost to himself. No,' Strong said firmly in that Scottish burr of his. 'Ranger Larsen is our man.'

'I agree,' Mackenzie said, knowing what the dead Sergeant Hawkins, the old sweat, had told him. His own investigations confirmed that too. 'It's this Larsen all right.'

'Yes.' Strong frowned. 'But here we have another problem, or several. One, where is Larsen and who is sheltering him? Two, even if and when we find him, which I think we will in due course, what if we discover that he is involved in these terrible murders – what did the press call the murderer? The Khaki Ripper?'

Mackenzie nodded his agreement and said quickly, 'It's interesting that since Larsen went to ground, the murders of uniformed women have ceased.'

Strong didn't seem to notice his comment. Slowly, fingers pursed together, he continued with, 'If we get that far, then I fear we have a real problem on our hands which has nothing to do with treachery and murder. It will be a matter of – what do they call it these days? – this new-fangled public relations.'

'How do you mean, sir?'

'This. So far the Rangers have been the only unit of the US Army to go into action in Europe. Soon they and their comrades will be involved in a very major action. But what will be the reaction here and in the United States? You can imagine the bad publicity we are going to get from both sides.'

'Yessir. But when we get that far,' Mackenzie answered swiftly, 'can't we hush the whole matter up? The Official Secrets Act and all that.'

Strong had shaken his head. ''Fraid not. Murder is a civil offence. Even in wartime and with the full weight of Mr Churchill behind us, I can't see how we could do it. The Press Hounds would be on to us like a shot. That woman at the *Daily Mirror* and her boss, Foot, it'd be what the Hun calls *ein gefundenes Fressen*.' He looked up enquiringly.

*Cunning chinless bugger*, Mackenzie had said to himself. Strong was testing his knowledge of colloquial German. Aloud he said, 'Yes, it certainly would. A real bone for the dog, if I may use an English phrase.'

Strong gave a little smile. 'You may, Mackenzie. All right, time is precious. Let us cut this interview short. I want you to liaise with that superintendent investigating the murders – the one from Scotland Yard. You will represent Intelligence. You must report to me *directly*, especially if the policeman comes up with something and wants to arrest people. There are policemen at Scotland Yard who are not disinclined to take a back-hander from the press for a hot tip. Well, soon-to-be Second Lieutenant Mackenzie, that's it. *An die Arbeit*, eh?'

'*An die Arbeit*,' he echoed, clicked to attention and marched out.

He followed that 'to work' order immediately. Over the next few days, he conferred with the superintendent, who was working all out to find the missing Ranger. Without success. He had interviewed the Wren, Daisy, in her hospital room, hoping that she might give him a clue, now that she was recovering. He had found her with an elderly staff colonel, who sported a monocle and looked and laughed like a horse. He had been very possessive and had kept patting the pillow and the sheet which covered her and Mackenzie could see that he could hardly keep himself from reaching under it and feeling her half-naked body.

But Daisy's interest in the opposite sex appeared to have diminished greatly since the episode with the crazy Ranger armed with a knife. Even the fact that the old officer had brought her hothouse grapes in purple crêpe paper, which must have cost a fortune, plus a bottle of champagne, didn't influence her. More than once, she had snapped almost angrily at him, 'Oh, Randy, will you stop your bloody games?' And he had accepted her rebuke like a naughty schoolboy with, 'Sorry, Daisy, but you have such a delightful – er – you know. Can't keep me hands off you, what.'

He had asked her point-blank if she had thought the Ranger might have possessed any secret knowledge of coming ops. Men often liked to impress women they wanted to bed with their importance by relating such matters.

She had shaken her head. 'No, the murderous swine was just an ordinary sort of squaddie after all, Sergeant. Looking back at it now, I think all he was interested in was getting my knickers down – and those of any other women he could lay his dirty paws on.'

At the mention of knickers, the old colonel's rheumy eyes had flickered excitedly and he'd exclaimed, 'By Gad, Daisy, you do say some naughty things. But I do like 'em.'

But while he investigated, Mackenzie, still shocked by the terrible events on the other side of the Channel at Dieppe, remembered the old sweat's last words to him as the former lay dying. They were still as much a mystery to him as they were on that fatal day. Yet they seemed important. Dying men, who knew they were dying, didn't waste time on unimportant matters. Why else did they cry for their mothers, the women who had brought them into this world? Wasn't it because they wanted the one who had been the most important person in their lives; the one who had given them the life which was being snuffed out so suddenly and so startlingly?

'He's got a tart,' the old sweat had choked, face twisted

into a grimace of pain . . . 'A tart with a snake.' Mackenzie
hadn't quite got the last word, as Hawkins had died in his
bloodstained hands, but he was sure that the little sergeant
had said, 'Dancer.' What did it mean? *A tart with a snake
who was a dancer.* Had he been confused, so shocked by
his terrible wound that his mind had been wandering?

But Hawkins had seemed lucid enough. So who was the
tart with the snake?

On and off for days as he had pursued his enquiries he
had puzzled over Hawkins' last words. A tart with a snake.
Why would a prostitute possess a reptile? Then the business
of her being a dancer, too. A whore, who was a dancer and
who possessed a snake. It didn't make sense. A couple of
days after he had interviewed Daisy in the hospital, he had
gone into one of the pubs near his barracks and had listened
idly to the chatter of the off-duty soldiers around him, as
they sipped their weak and scarce wartime beer.

As usual with soldiers, the main topic of conversation
was 'subject number one', as they called it – sex. He had
heard their stories before. They were always the same: the
details of their conquests of the female species. *So I got
her in this corner and I sez to her, I'm gonna give you
something you've never had before, luv. And d'yer know
what the cheeky cow answered? Like leprosy, big boy.* It
was that sort of thing. Idly he listened as he drank his
beer and pondered his own problems until he had begun
to realize that the soldiers' slang for women, 'bint', 'Judy'
and, in particular, the word 'tart', didn't mean they were
talking about prostitutes. 'Tart' was just another piece of
Army slang. So Hawkins hadn't been talking of a whore
who possessed a snake, but an ordinary woman.

That realization cleared his mind. So it was that at
nine the following morning he was on the phone to the
rather pompous-sounding keeper of the reptile house at

Whipsnade Zoo asking, 'Is it permitted, sir, for a private person to keep a snake in wartime?'

'Of course,' the keeper answered, as if he were asking a very foolish question. 'Why not? It's a free country, so they tell me. The only problem for someone keeping a reptile in wartime is the availability of foodstuffs for the creature. Snakes don't eat everything, you know. They're very choosy,' he added testily.

'How do you mean, sir?'

'Well, they don't particularly fancy Woolton Pie or Snoek, you know.' He was referring to wartime dishes which were supposed to fill the half-starved, long-suffering British population. 'They like fruit, tropical fruits, bananas and the like, the occasional chicken or even rat, if needs be.'

'But such things are impossible to get, sir,' Mackenzie objected, 'even on the black market.'

'Not quite,' the prissy voice on the other end at Whipsnade said, 'Certain people are allowed special rations if they keep reptiles for research purposes, for instance, or their profession—'

'Profession!' Mackenzie interjected urgently, remembering the dying Hawkins' reference to the 'dancer'. 'Dancers – exotic dancers, for example?'

The keeper seemed embarrassed. 'Yes, that sort of person might be included in the special ration group. I suppose we need that sort of woman in—'

But Mackenzie was no longer listening. Half an hour later he and the superintendent from Scotland Yard were poring over the list of snake owners in London who were receiving special food rations, eyes focused on a single profession – *exotic dancer*.

# Five

The Ace of Spades was packed. Every table in the little Chelsea nightclub was occupied by officers of virtually every Allied nation – British, American, Free French, Poles, even a few Luxembourgers. All of them were accompanied by women, flushed and a little excited, smoking cigarette after cigarette with hands that trembled, as if they couldn't wait for the main event of the evening – sex.

Sweating waiters hurried back and forth, carrying silver trays heavy with glasses and black-market champagne in buckets, beads of water trickling down the bottles.

The noise was terrific. On the raised platform in the centre of the club, a big Negro, the sweat glistening on his fat black face, as if it had been greased, was slamming away at his drums, while a skinny little white saxophonist played 'The White Cliffs of Dover' – badly. None of the guests minded. They were laughing and shouting at one another, the noise they made punctuated by the wild screams of the drunken whores.

Superintendent Cherrill took it all in and sniffed, 'Well, I suppose they ought to have a bit of fun before they get the chop. But my guess is that there's more black-market activity going on this night than you'd find on any street corner in the East End. Worse than spivs some of 'em.'

Mackenzie, now wearing his new officer's uniform,

complete with the one pip of a second lieutenant, yelled in the middle-aged policeman's ear, 'You're a moralist, Super.'

The latter shook his greying head. 'Ner. Just a mean suspicious old flatfoot.'

A greasy-looking waiter appeared out of nowhere. 'No tables, gentlemen. Sorry.' His accent was foreign, Mackenzie noted immediately. He pulled out a note. 'Ten bob help?' he queried.

The greasy-looking waiter flashed him a toothy smile. 'I think I have just discovered two empty seats, gentlemen.'

The superintendent frowned, but when he saw the two free chairs were at the back of the crowded, smoke-filled room near the wall, he didn't object. As a good policeman he always liked to have his back to the wall; it was safer that way.

They nodded to the two Polish officers who occupied the other chairs at the table. The Poles bowed stiffly in their fashion and then went back to their giggling whores, the younger of the Poles already occupied with trying to get his hand up his girl's short skirt.

The waiter said, 'Drinks, gentlemen – cocktails, champagne—'

'Beer,' the superintendent cut him off sharply.

'But we don't serve,' the waiter began, till he saw the look on the cop's granite face and changed his mind. 'Beer,' he said and started to force his way through the sweating shouting throng.

At the next table a drunken Yank, collar ripped open, overseas cap pushed to the back of his head, was giving a passable imitation of President Roosevelt giving one of his 'fireside chats' to the American nation, declaring in the previous year that the USA would never go to war: 'Mah good friends, ah hate wah, Sissie hates wah, Buzzie hates wah – we all hate wah. I'll never send you boys overseas.' The drunken officer resumed his normal voice, crying, 'And where are we, boys?'

As one, as if they had done this before, his equally drunken comrades yelled, *'We're overseas in a frigging war!'*

Mackenzie laughed. The superintendent frowned. No one else seemed to have heard. It didn't matter, if they had. For now the noise was dying away and all eyes were being focused on the tiny stage.

A big-bosomed blonde in tall wooden-heeled platform shoes, a tight black silk skirt that emphasized her curves and a white silk blouse from which her breasts threatened to explode at any moment, had tottered up on to the platform. But it was the object that was curled around her neck and shoulders which had caught the attention of her drunken noisy audience.

It was a large glistening speckled snake, which, apparently upset by the audience, had opened its mouth to reveal its fangs and the long divided tongue which flickered in and out dangerously. Here and there women gasped with surprise or disgust. Not the men. For now the big blonde was gyrating her ample hips, her breasts trembling like puddings, sweat breaking out on her face, running in streaks down the powder. On her shoulders the big snake seemed to join in swaying back and forth too, fangs flickering, dark eyes full of danger.

'Take it off!' the drunken American officer yelled. He meant the blonde's blouse probably. She thought otherwise. She caught the snake and cuddled it between her breasts, aiming tiny little kisses at its mouth. Women cried 'ugh!' in disgust and the men in the audience went strangely silent, as if they had been attacked by a sudden unease, which they couldn't quite explain.

Behind the woman grinding her hips lasciviously, hugging the snake ever closer to those massive breasts of hers, the drummer started to thud his drum in a sombre regular rhythm, while the saxophonist made his instrument wail in a kind of primeval dirge. Slowly the blonde started to release one of her breasts, pointing her carmine-painted nipple in the direction of the snake's fangs, so that the snake seemed almost to be licking it. A deep gasp rose from the audience and Mackenzie told himself that she was getting them turned on all right. Now he was sure she was poor Sergeant Hawkins' 'dancer'. But where was Madame de Paula – as she was billed outside the club – friend of the missing Irishman O'Corrigan?

Now the blonde was thrusting the snake downwards. In the awed silence which had fallen over the audience, they could hear the slither of its scales along the silk of her blouse and then on to the skirt, which had been hitched up to reveal the black stocking tops, her garters and the fat white flesh of her thighs. Next to Mackenzie, the superintendent said, 'If she carries on like that, they'll prosecute her.' But even his tone was excited, as if he didn't have himself quite under control.

By this time the snake's head was almost parallel with her stomach and what lay below it. Mackenzie, watching entranced, reasoned many of those present in the audience would have no idea of phallic symbolism and all that kind of Freudian mumbo-jumbo. But they wouldn't need a crystal ball to figure what the snake was supposed to represent and what was intended. He told himself this wasn't an erotic dancer; this was a bloody pornographic one!

The drum was thudding ever louder now. The dancer was becoming wilder. The snake's fangs flickered out and in from its gaping pink jaws, swifter and swifter. The very blue air of the place seemed to quiver with passion and raw sex. The blonde's whole body appeared to shake. Her plump belly moved in and out frantically. She threw back her head, saliva trickling down the sides of her wide-open mouth. Sweat poured off her. She clenched the snake ever closer to her loins. She started to curse terrible obscenities. She mimed the sex act with the snake.

The audience loved it. Their fists clenched. The women let their mouths drop as if in wonder. The whores' eyes glittered hard. Even the drunken Americans were silent, totally preoccupied by the sight of the half-naked woman and the slimy snake, coiled about her loins, as if it now possessed the woman and had taken over.

Suddenly – startlingly – the blonde broke into great shuddering jerks. It was as if she was reaching a climax. Perhaps she was. She grabbed the snake roughly. She encircled its slimy coils and pressed them with all her strength. Meaningless words and groans came from her suddenly slack lips. Mackenzie, as entranced as the rest by the spectacle, thought he heard her groan, 'Oh, my God!' as if she couldn't believe what was happening to her. It might all be fake, he told himself afterwards when he got to know her, but at that moment in the cellar bar, it didn't seem like it to him.

The light went dim. The drummer ceased his thudding. The lights went out. The audience didn't move. They were still too entranced. The lights went on again. The audience still didn't move. It was as if they were frozen thus for eternity. Then the waiters, ready for orders, started to make their way through the crowded tables beaming winningly at their guests and, out of the corner of his eye, Mackenzie saw the big red-headed civilian holding the street coat ready for the blonde to cover her sweat-lathered half nakedness.

For a moment he didn't believe the evidence of his own eyes. Then he knew it had to be him. The exotic dancer *was* the girl who had sheltered him. And that red hair. It *had* to be O'Corrigan!

He didn't hesitate. He nudged the policeman in the ribs – hard. 'It's him,' he hissed. 'O'Corrigan!'

Then things happened fast. The two of them pushed through the throng. The greasy-looking waiter was sent flying, cursing in Italian, as his tray containing the fake French champagne went clattering down with him. Women screamed. A burly Yank tried to bar their way. 'Hey buddy!' he cried drunkenly. 'What's the big idea . . .' He didn't finish. The superintendent gave him a fist in his fat belly. He, too, went down spluttering.

Wildly O'Corrigan looked around for some way of escape. Paula unwound the snake from her shoulders, as if she were going to throw it at the two men. It dropped to the floor. Tamely it slithered beneath the nearest table. A woman fainted. Another clambered hurriedly on to the table, scattering glasses on all sides, lifting her skirts up to reveal she wasn't a true blonde. She started to scream hysterically as well.

But Mackenzie didn't give the fugitive a chance to escape again. He pulled out the little pistol he always kept in his trouser pocket these days and pointed it at the big Irishman's heart. 'Hold it there, O'Corrigan!' he cried above the pandemonium. 'Don't do anything foolish.'

Tamely O'Corrigan started to raise his hands in token of surrender, his shoulders slumped slightly, as if he'd had enough, was sick of running. Next moment, the policeman had pulled his arms down behind his back. Neatly he clicked the cuffs on, while next to the prisoner Madame Paula looked on in helpless silence . . .

# Book Four: The Escape Plot

'My experience is that the gentlemen who are the best behaved and the most sleek are those who are doing the mischief. We cannot be too sure of anybody.'

*Field Marshal Lord Ironside. WWII*

# One

Larsen lay naked on the bed. Thoughtfully he fingered his half-erection, as he went through his plan once again. He had already gone through most of the practical details. He could jam his bedroom door easily. His window needed a mere five more minutes' work on it and then he could get on to the little balcony with the drainpipe to the garden below within easy reach.

He paused for a moment and felt a sense of pleasure surge through his hairy loins. In a way, he told himself, he would be combining sexual enjoyment with the escape. For he knew he had to escape; he couldn't rely on the dagoes. If anything went wrong with *their* escape plans, they'd dump him like a ton of bricks. He'd be too much of a political embarrassment to the fancy pants who ran the embassy.

That morning the dago faggot with the cocaine habit had briefed him on how the dagoes were going to get him to Germany via Ireland. He had listened attentively, picking their brains and wondering if they would give him some dough before he set out rather than afterwards when he finally reached Germany – *If you ever do, buddy* – a harsh little cynical voice had sneered at the back of his mind.

Now and again he had thrown a covert glance at the faggot just to check his facial expression; it might give him some clue to what the dago was thinking. But the faggot was playing the game with his cards close to his

171

chest. Still Larsen had an uneasy feeling that the faggot was having him on and it made his intention to look after his own escape stronger. But where was he going to get the necessary dough from if he were to make a break for it independently of the Spaniards?

It had come to him during the night with the 100 per cent certainty of an overwhelming vision. *The dame!* The dames they brought him when he demanded 'a little female company, Miguel' and 'you know, kinda a bit of relief'. The whores always had money. Moreover they came and went by taxi; and a taxi could function not only as an escape car, it, too, would have money in it: the limey driver's fares.

The more he thought about his own personal escape plan, the more the killer liked it. Now he knew he could trust no one. The Good Lord had put him on this earth to promote the Good and fight the Evil. But he had found out as he had grown into manhood that the Good Lord had not realized just how wicked his creatures were, especially those of the female sex. Even those who were naturally good and followed His ways and guidance as he did would end up corrupted by those she-devils with their flashing eyes, fleshly evil charms and demonic vulvas, flaunted before His poor weak men.

But it had gone further than that. There were those of God's own male creatures who were decadent and corrupt even without being tempted by these damned whores. The dagoes were like that. God in heaven! Larsen's face contorted into a mad grimace at the thought of the faggot, who he knew would betray him at the drop of a hat. Surely God would not hesitate a moment if there was an opportunity to eradicate such devil's spawn from His universe?

With an effort of sheer willpower Larsen calmed himself,

pulled himself together and quelled the red-hot rage that had abruptly risen at the thought of how the Good Lord was being deceived and betrayed by such abysmal creatures, male and female. He told himself he had to keep calm. It was the only way he could carry out his plan. He knew now he would never reach Germany; he had nothing more to offer the Krauts. He would fool the lot of them. He wouldn't even go to Southern Ireland. That country was full of potato-eating papist Micks anyway. No, wasn't Liverpool on that coast and didn't fleets of US merchantmen sail for the States from the limey port? Hell, surely a guy called 'Swede' Larsen could find a berth on one of those merchantmen, manned by Swedes, especially if he had a handful of good old greenbacks in his jeans.

Larsen relaxed on the bed. In the mirror opposite, he admired his muscular young body and that great devil's instrument that those damned whores always craved for – to their cost. Mechanically, his eyes closed, his mind full of delightful images, he started to work his fist up and down . . .

Two miles away O'Corrigan had calmed down. He had seen that his captors had treated Paula well enough before she had been led away by a policewoman. They had given her a cup of strong tea, laced with rum, a cigarette, and the burly policewoman with the cropped hair and heavy jaw had actually stroked her hand gently to soothe her until she had ceased weeping. Now sipping a whisky, surprisingly provided by the superintendent, he had commenced speaking, the rage vanished from his long Irish face, to be replaced by a look of tired resignation.

'I know I shouldn't have done it,' he said softly. 'But I'd had enough – for a long time, ever since I was hit in the desert. I just couldn't stand the bullshit any longer, the kind that led to that balls-up recently at Dieppe.'

Mackenzie nodded his understanding. He knew what O'Corrigan meant. There were still thousands of men in the UK who had never fired a shot in anger since the British Expeditionary Force had been run out of Europe so shamefully at Dunkirk. Since '40 the British Army had, in general, settled down to a kind of peace-time soldiering of bullshit and drill and yet more drill. He could understand why fighting soldiers like O'Corrigan had rebelled.

The superintendent had apparently understood too. He said, 'Don't worry about it, son. That's all in the past. You'll probably get stripped of your rank, but that'll be about it. There'll be no clink for you, trust me.'

Obviously O'Corrigan did, for he said, 'I'd like to tell you something. I know where that swine Larsen is hiding out.'

'*What?*' Mackenzie exclaimed.

'Where he's hiding out. But I'll say this now. It's going to be one hell of a job to get him out of his lair.'

'What do you mean, son?' the superintendent asked. 'If he's in this country—'

'He's in London,' O'Corrigan interrupted the policeman. 'Not a million miles from where we are now. All the same, you wouldn't be able to get him out of his hiding place. If you tried it'd cause one hell of a stink. I don't think even Mr Churchill would risk it.'

Puzzled as he was and yet eager to get his hands on the American killer, Mackenzie said, 'All right let's have it, O'Corrigan. Where is he?'

'The Spanish legation here in London.' O'Corrigan answered and finished off the rest of his tea with a sort of angry flourish.

Mackenzie realized the import of the Irishman's words immediately. 'So he betrayed the Dieppe op to get sanctuary from the Spaniards, who passed on the info to the

Jerries, who were waiting for us when we hit the beaches over there. So the bastard is responsible for the destruction of a whole Canadian division, not to speak of the death of his comrades in the Rangers and the Commandos who trained them.'

O'Corrigan nodded. 'Something like that.'

'But how do you know he's there?' the superintendent persisted, while Mackenzie lapsed momentarily into silence, feeling angry and bitter at what the Yank killer had done.

Swiftly O'Corrigan explained how he and Paula had observed the Spanish Embassy for several nights and how they had seen the London whores smuggled in for Larsen's perverted pleasures.

'Brass-necked bastards aren't they, the Spaniards?' the superintendent commented when O'Corrigan was finished. 'But I suppose that's part of their diplomatic immunity.' His face fell as he said the words and realized exactly what that immunity meant: they couldn't get their hands on the wanted man. He could hide there for the duration of the war.

O'Corrigan must have been able to read the middle-aged cop's mind, for he said quietly, 'I have a plan.'

'What . . . what kind of plan?' Mackenzie asked surprised. He'd thought that O'Corrigan, after what he had been through at the hands of the military authorities, would have been primarily concerned with saving his own hide. After all he wasn't even an Englishman, but a national of a neutral country, Southern Ireland.

'Yes, I want to get the bastard if it's the last thing I ever do,' he rasped, eyes suddenly blazing furiously.

'But what can you do that we can't?' Mackenzie snapped.

O'Corrigan laughed in that wild brash Irish fashion. 'Go

beyond the bounds of legality, as I've always done. That's why I'm here, isn't it? In the bloody nick.'

'Go on,' the superintendent urged.

Swiftly the Irishman told him the plan he had been working on for the last week or so, the words tumbling out as if he couldn't get them off his chest quickly enough.

When he was finished, a heavy silence fell on the spartan room, broken only by the clink of the jailer's keys outside as he plodded down the corridor on his official business. It was the superintendent who broke it first. 'But even if your lady friend could get herself picked for the night by the Spaniards and smuggled inside to this Larsen bloke, won't it be damned dangerous for her?'

'When I get my hands on him, it'll be bloody dangerous for him,' O'Corrigan growled.

The policeman ignored the interruption. 'After all, O'Corrigan, you know that Larsen murdered at least three poor women.'

'But they were in uniform. My Paula won't be.'

The superintendent wasn't convinced, but he dropped his objection. 'All right, suppose the Spaniards pick her for a little bit of, eh –' he hesitated; he didn't want to offend the prisoner – 'slap-and-tickle, how do you intend to get into the embassy? Naturally, we can't. There'd be all hell to pay if officers of Scotland Yard were found illegally in the legation. We don't want any trouble with Spain in the Med. We've got enough bloody trouble there already.'

'Well, superintendent, I'll be driving the taxi that takes her to the embassy and the Spaniards usually let the taxi driver wait outside till Larsen has –' he frowned, as if he were realizing for the first time what he was letting his Paula in for – 'has finished with the whore. But this particular driver, yours truly, won't be sitting in his cab having a fly kip. He'll be going up the outside of the embassy to get into Larsen's bedroom.' Suddenly his tough Irish face broke into a wary smile. 'After all, superintendent, I am Commando-trained. I can be up that outer wall in a brace of shakes.'

'All right.' Mackenzie spoke for the first time since O'Corrigan had revealed his daring plan. 'Remember the Spaniards will have watchmen, too. They'll probably be soldiers in civvies like our own people at embassies abroad.'

His objection didn't worry O'Corrigan. He eyed Mackenzie, seemed to notice the green flash of the Intelligence Corps he wore on his shoulder, and said, 'I always thought Intelligence wallahs were nervous nellies, always worrying about things that might never happen. Don't worry, Lieutenant. I think I can take care of any wop watchman.' He doubled a fist like a steam shovel to emphasize his point.

'Let's get on with it,' the superintendent snapped, as if he were irritated. Perhaps he was, at the thought of this delicate operation being carried out by amateurs in the form of British soldiers instead of his professionals of New Scotland Yard. 'OK, you get in, you nab the bugger. Now tell me this, how are you going to get him out? He's a big bastard by all accounts. He could be screaming blue murder, waking the whole embassy.'

Mackenzie nodded his agreement. He knew that O'Corrigan was risking his life in his attempt to kidnap Larsen and bring him to justice. But still his plan was too daring. There were too many imponderables to it.

O'Corrigan looked at their faces in the poor yellow light cast by the single naked bulb of the little prison office. Outside in the area of the cells, a plaintive voice said, 'If you don't let me out soon, I'm going to piss mesen.' The jailer answered back with a laconic, 'Well, then go ahead,

177

piss yersen. It might make yer smell a bit better. Now shut up that racket and go ter sleep.'

'Well,' he said slowly, perhaps mocking his two interrogators, 'I could kill the bastard there and then in the bedroom and have done with it. But I won't,' he added swiftly. 'I want to see him brought to trial and, with a bit o' luck and the permission of His Majesty, be witness to him dangling on the end of a rope, having the life choked out of his evil body.'

'Now enough of that, O'Corrigan,' the superintendent snapped sharply. 'Let Mr Pierrepoint, the official hangman, take care of that. How do you propose to get him out without waking the whole damned place?'

'Chloroform,' O'Corrigan answered simply.

'Excellent,' the superintendent exclaimed. 'Just the job, knock him out.' He eyed the Irishman's big, broad-shouldered frame. 'And lug him down the outside of the building.'

'Yes. Me and Paula has got it all worked out. The two of us could manage him with a rope – Paula's pretty strong, she needs to be, lugging that bloody heavy snake of hers around. Let him into the taxi and then, with a bit of luck, we're home and dry.'

'Yes,' the superintendent agreed, warming to the plan. 'We can have some of my lads in plain clothes hidden near the taxi. Once you get Larsen that far, O'Corrigan, you can rest assured that you'll have no more trouble.' He yawned wearily. ''Bout time for some shut-eye.' He nodded to the desk sergeant, sitting behind his high desk like some Dickensian counting-house clerk, his penny wooden pen at the ready. 'Book him, Sarge,' he ordered. 'But don't lock the cell door, and see he's comfy.' He turned to O'Corrigan. 'Just a formality, O'Corrigan. But officially you're still a deserter and a wanted man.'

Now very tired himself, O'Corrigan nodded his understanding. 'Glad to get my head down as well,' he commented. 'It feels as if I haven't shut my eyes for ages.' Now he yawned.

The sergeant scribbled something and then pressed the bell on his desk. The flat-footed jailer, his braces dangling, shuffled in and said, 'All right, follow me.' He jingled his bunch of keys.

'I'll come with you,' the superintendent volunteered, 'and see everything's hunky-dory.'

O'Corrigan nodded to Mackenzie and then they were gone, leaving Mackenzie alone with the sergeant, who now was busy scribbling in his big leather-bound ledger, and the Ministry of Works clock on the wall, ticking away the seconds of their lives with metallic inexorability. It was only then that the thought struck the young Intelligence officer. What if Larsen suddenly went crazy during the attempt? He'd already murdered those other women and mutilated them so cruelly. Would he do the same to O'Corrigan's 'exotic dancer'?

# Two

The diplomat was very businesslike. He stood at the corner of Shaftesbury Avenue, ignoring the banter of the Americans and the prostitutes, the ones in the doorways flashing the torches held under their chins to display their wares. He discussed the terms with the taxi driver, who was obviously the woman's pimp. He couldn't see him well in the blackout, but it didn't matter. He didn't want to see him. Indeed, it was extremely distasteful to him to have to deal with such decadent trash. He said, 'You must tell her that her client will demand certain things from her—'

'Extras, Guv?'

'Yes, I suppose so. Tell her she must comply. She will be well paid.'

'No vaseline jobs, Guv,' the muffled taxi driver said. 'Nuthin' like that. It hurts, she sez. But anything else, as long as yer pays.'

A couple of drunken American soldiers staggered by. They saw the little group next to the static water tank and said, 'Heard about the new utility knickers, friend? One Yank and they're off!' They went on their way laughing uproariously. The diplomat was puzzled and the cab driver growled, 'Ruddy Yanks. Think they own the ruddy world.'

'*Bueno*,' the diplomat concluded. '*Y hecho.*'

'Eh?'

'No matter. You will bring the woman to the place just after midnight. My people will await you. Be discreet. Here –' he reached into his wallet and brought out four crisp white five pound notes. 'There will be a *propina* – tip – for you personally when you fetch her. Clear?'

'Clear, sir.' The taxi driver's tone changed immediately when he saw the twenty pounds. 'A pony,' he said to himself. 'Christ, I thought he was just renting her, not buying her.'

'What?' the diplomat asked. He was always puzzled by the language of the English working classes; it was not at all like the English he had once studied at the University of Madrid.

'Nothing, sir. Just saying thank you, sir. I'll be there as ordered. You can rely on me. I'll be off, sir, to pick up the little lady.'

The diplomat nodded and the driver engaged first gear. Slowly he started to draw away, leaving the diplomat standing there, the encounter already forgotten, save that he would have liked to wash his hands immediately. They felt dirty after dealing with such common trash, especially the English common trash. They simply didn't know their place like their kind in Spain did. General Franco had soon taught them that after his victory of 1939.

He dismissed the problem of the impertinent English working classes and concentrated on the Larsen Problem once more. All morning the American had been demanding he should be given a woman this very night. He was going wild, caged in his bedroom, cut off from the world without even a woman to pleasure him. What did he have to enjoy himself with? Hell, the only stuff he had to read was in 'goddam dago'. The diplomat flushed angrily at the thought. The American had had the audacity to use those very words. He knew 'dago' was only a corruption of the Spanish name 'Diego', but its use was an insult to him and all Hispanics, and the Yankee pig knew it.

He stopped. A slim blond boy had stepped out of the doorway of a bombed-out shop. He could vaguely make out the warning sign above the brick rubble: *Warning, Unexploded Bomb.* The warning seemed not to worry the boy; perhaps he and his kind felt safer where the police wouldn't bother them. 'I wonder if I could trouble you for a light, sir?' the boy asked in a polite, well-educated manner.

Instinctively he reached for his lighter; then changed his mind immediately. The boy was handsome and very tempting. But why had he picked on him? Was it a police trap? He could see the headline already. *Foreign diplomat arrested in sex scandal!* 'No,' he answered swiftly. 'I'm afraid I don't smoke, young man.'

The boy said fawningly, 'Perhaps, sir, you could let me help you? You seem a gentleman of a kindly nature.' He reached out a hand and touched the diplomat's arm lightly. 'I aim to please.'

The diplomat wrenched his own arm away hurriedly. 'I'm afraid you can't help. I must be on my way.'

'Yessir. Of course, sir,' the boy said, in no way offended. 'But if you ever do change your mind, sir, you can always find me here as soon as it is dark. You understand, sir?'

The diplomat did, only too well. But he didn't respond. Shaking a little at the encounter, he hurried away from temptation, if that was what it was. Or was it something else? Had the police followed him to this disgusting area and, knowing his little failing, that tiny weakness of the flesh, as he was wont to call it in certain circles back in Madrid, tried to entrap him?

And why would they attempt that? His arrest would not lead to a prosecution in a British court. After all, he possessed diplomatic immunity. No, all they could use a situation like that for was in order to blackmail him. And why should the English police attempt to blackmail him? The answer was obvious. They knew about the fugitive hidden in the legation and wanted him to ensure that Larsen be forced out of the embassy so that they could arrest him.

Faintly in the distance he could hear the first dread wail which indicated that the Germans were coming to bomb London once again. As he heard the sirens, he remembered the blond boy in the doorway of the ruined shop with the warning sign behind in the rubble. *Warning, Unexploded Bomb*. He stopped for a moment and licked his suddenly dry lips. An idea was beginning to uncurl at the back of his mind like the coils of some deadly snake, just about to strike.

These days in London, raids resulting in the death of unknowns happened every night. Cases of unexpected bodies being found were reported daily in the press. Nobody paid much attention to them. They happened too frequently. Sometimes there were as many as a couple of hundred a night. The victims, a mess of jumbled limbs, often without heads, were buried in mass graves and their plight forgotten in an instant. In such cases the police and the civilian authorities of the ARP carried out perfunctory searches and that was that. As always, they were merely another example of total war.

He considered. What if he decided to solve his prob-lem with the damned Yankee in a similar manner? The ambassador wouldn't object. Indeed, he had stated cat-egorically right from the outset that he wanted to know nothing about the Larsen business. He didn't want to jeopardize his diplomatic career for the sake of a spy and possible murderer. So the business would be left to him.

The sudden belch of cherry flame to the east alerted him to his danger. The English flak guns were opening up. It would be ironic if he were killed by the soldiers of the very nation which had just awarded him the German Cross in Gold for his efforts on Germany's behalf in the Dieppe business. He moved on, his mind full of his new plan, while behind him the Germans pressed home their bombing attack . . .

O'Corrigan took Paula's hand in his. He was a man not given to sentimentality; he had been a soldier too long. The war had brutalized him like it did most young men. Faced with violent death at almost any moment, the young men of the PBI – the Poor Bloody Infantry – took their pleasures where they found them, swiftly, passionately, and without love. There was no time for love. Love would mean a commitment that they couldn't honour. All the same, O'Corrigan felt for Paula. She had been good to him, a soldier on the run with no prospects, even now, save death on the battlefield. For O'Corrigan reasoned that when this Larsen business was over and done with, the powers-that-be would ship him off to the front again as soon as possible. He knew too much and Anglo-American relations couldn't be endangered in order to ensure that justice was done to him, a broken-down infantryman, who had never known how to toe the line. Besides, he was an Irishman, wasn't he, and in the eyes of the English establishment that said everything, didn't it.

So he held out his hand and said, 'Paula, darling, you won't take any serious risks, will you? If the worst comes to the worst, we'll simply let the bastard get away with it, *macushla*.'

Tough as she was and, as old Sergeant Hawkins would have said, had 'had more fucks than I've had good dinners', she was moved. She took his hand and pressed it hard.

'Silly old bugger,' she said, the tears glinting in her
red-rimmed eyes. ''Course I won't. I know how to handle
the type.'

He nodded and asked, 'Will you let him – you know?'
Suddenly as tough and as hard-boiled as he was, O'Corrigan
felt himself blushing.

'*Fuck me?*' she completed the question. She laughed. 'Of
course I will if it'll tame the bastard till you get your big
paws on him, Rory.' She shrugged and her tired old breasts
sailed upwards behind the thin material of her 'art-silk'
blouse. 'Anything to get him out of that house, into clink.'
She pressed his big paw harder, almost lovingly. 'Anything
that'll clear you, Rory.'

'Thanks, Paula. I don't know what I'd have done—'

'Shut up, you silly big Mick!' she interrupted him.
'Don't go all Irish and sentimental on me. Yer'll have
me singing "Danny Boy" in half a mo.'

He forced a grin. 'I don't even know the words,' he
said.

She shared his grin.

From the shadows, Superintendent Cherrill whispered,
'All right, O'Corrigan, better get going. Remember, my
people won't be far away, when you need them.'

'Understood,' the Irishman replied, keeping his gaze to
the front. The traffic, mostly military, was thinning out
now. Even the Yanks looking for a girl for the night
were vanishing off the streets. London was settling down
for another night at war, with the civilians praying that
their sleep wouldn't be disturbed by another air raid.
The old apprehension, excitement, sense of adventure at
the prospect of a dramatic air battle over the capital had
vanished. Only the kids looked forward to an air raid
these days. If the raid lasted after midnight they didn't
have to go to school till midday. Otherwise for the adults,

raids just meant another burden on their miserable, shabby, half-starved lives.

As the old cab moved away, Mackenzie turned to the policeman. 'What do you think, Super? About his chances, once he's inside the embassy, if he does manage to get inside.'

'Well he's a tough bastard and he can fight like all Micks,' the policeman replied. He shrugged. 'But once he's inside that embassy, it'll be as if he's in a foreign country, an *enemy* foreign country, with every man's hand against him . . . and remember that Yank Larsen's a cold-blooded killer.' He shrugged again. 'We'll see. Now come along, Mackenzie, we can't stand here like two old biddies gossiping . . .'

Larsen looked at himself in the full-length nineteenth-century mirror. He was naked and he had a full erection. He looked at it and said to himself, 'Now what'll she say when she sees that?' He smiled at himself in the mirror; it wasn't pleasant. 'A whore like that has seen a lot of cocks. But I bet my bottom dollar she's never seen one like that.' He stroked his ugly engorged penis and was tempted. But that inner voice that had been guiding him a lot these last few days snapped harshly. 'Stop that!'

He took his hand away as if it had been suddenly burned.

'Don't you realize that is the Devil's work?' the voice thundered inside his head. 'Save your seed. Don't waste it. Do you understand?'

'I understand, sir.' He hesitated as usual about that 'sir'. For he didn't know whether it was God speaking to him or one of His subordinates. It was someone in authority, that he knew. So he thought it better to call the voice 'sir'.

Larsen took one last look at himself in the mirror. The erection was vanishing. Still he thought even in its present state the penis looked good. He turned hurriedly, knowing he mustn't offend the voice again, if he wanted to be saved in this wanton world.

Now he made a last survey of his escape route. The stout chair was next to the door of his bedroom. Of course, the spics had the key on the outside. But once he had the girl inside, he could block the door with the chair. The window was already free of locks and bolts. Indeed he had already been outside on the little balustrade to check whether he could reach the drainage pipe, which he'd use now to reach the ground. Once he got that far, he'd pull his spare pair of socks over his shoes to ensure he'd make no noise approaching the taxi. If the driver cut up rough, Larsen grinned at the thought, well, the knife would soon put him in his place. Indeed, he felt he'd enjoy cutting someone up, even if he were a man and not one of those whores in uniform.

He slipped his singlet over his head and pulled on his underpants. That's all he'd need to welcome the whore. Of course he could have remained naked. But that wouldn't have been so much fun. He wanted to strip off in front of her and hear her gasp when she saw the size of his dong. Brother, was she in for a surprise! He rubbed his flaccid member for a second and then, remembering the voice's warning, pulled his hand away swiftly. Outside he heard the sound of a vehicle slowing down. He hurried to the window and pulled the blackout curtain a little to one side.

It was the taxi pulling up under the trees opposite. The spic faggot always insisted the cab driver should 'deposit', as the Spaniard called it, the whore there. 'One has to be discreet, you know,' he would say in that fruitcake manner of his, the faggot! Larsen pulled a face. Then he peered through the silvery darkness trying to catch a glimpse of the whore as she emerged from the cab.

By the light of the moon, scudding in and out of the clouds, he could see she was blonde – the whores always were – and big. He didn't mind that. He'd tamed bigger women. Besides, he liked to get his hands on a woman with plenty of sinful flesh and ensure that she got the punishment she deserved. He strained his eyes, as the diplomat's watchman said something to the taxi driver. He was the smaller of the watchmen, Larsen noted automatically – easy meat – as he managed to make out that the whore was wearing some sort of small hat. Then for a moment the moon cast its silvery light fully on the whore's headgear. 'Holy cow!' Larsen exclaimed involuntarily, his heart abruptly beating very fast. It was a kind of military cap. Then the moon vanished behind the clouds once more and he could no longer make out any further details of her clothing.

He swallowed with difficulty. Did that military-type cap mean she was one of those sinful broads who were a disgrace to their uniform, fucking around as if they were full-time professionals and not members of a force fighting for good against evil? Suddenly he was very confused. He let the curtain slip back into place. Would she have to be punished? What was he going to do? He clasped his hands together as if in prayer and posed that overwhelming question.

No answer came. The voice inside his head remained stubbornly silent. He was on his own. Almost unconsciously he started to reach for the knife . . .

# Three

'Now what do you say to this, honey?' Larsen said, the saliva drooling down the sides of his slack, wet mouth. He indicated the bulge in his shorts.

Paula wasn't impressed, but she daren't show it. She already knew that she was dealing with a murderer, but she hadn't realized he was mad too; and this one was certainly a real looney; and she'd met a lot of looney men in her time. She decided it would be safer to play along with him until Rory was ready. 'It . . . it looks . . . *huge!*' she attempted to gush.

'You betcha, baby. There aren't many around as big as this.' He pulled the shorts down in one swift movement to reveal the ugly red penis of which he was so proud. Larsen was disappointed that she wasn't in the military, but for the moment he was content with having sex with the whore and letting the watchmen below know that he was in business. He'd creak the bedsprings for the listeners till they went back to their usual dozing and then he'd take off, confident that the spics would be off guard.

He bent down on her as she lay on the bed, still fully clothed. 'Let's see the tits first,' he said thickly, the spittle dropping disgustingly on her upturned face. 'Got to see the tits!'

'Let me take—' He didn't give her a chance to finish her request. Instead he reached down his big paw and ripped the blouse away from her chest to reveal her breasts. Next moment he was suckling her left nipple crazily like a milk-hungry wild animal.

Now Paula started to become really afraid. The man was totally crazy, she told herself apprehensively, as he stopped his suckling and began cupping her breasts with his hands, stopping every now and again to squeeze her big nipples painfully.

'Please—' she began.

He wasn't even listening. 'Let's stop the prelims,' he cut into her words. 'Let Pappa have a look at that big pussy o' yourn.'

Suddenly she realized she had to fight back. Rory couldn't be far away now. Frenzied she raised her hips and with her right leg tried to knee him. He didn't even notice. With one hand holding her down, he pulled off her knickers and with the other he ripped her legs apart. She shrieked. He hit her across the mouth with his open hand. Her head jerked painfully to one side. 'Shut it, bitch!' he hissed, face set in a pink leer, his eyes bulging crazily.

She felt his gross thing between her thighs. Now she was not prepared to lie back and let it happen till Rory came up. Suddenly she hated him. He wasn't going to have his way with her, just like that. 'OK, OK, OK, honey,' he was chanting like a prayer to a god unknown, 'here we go . . . go . . . go!' He spread her legs even wider, gaping at her exposed labia. 'Love this . . . oh, bitch, love this!' He guided his penis towards her vulva. She struggled and struggled, gasping for breath, her face scarlet with the effort. But he held both her hands easily with his one huge paw. He sighed abruptly with pleasure. 'Oh, my God!' he breathed as he felt himself slide into her.

'*No!*' she screamed with the last of her strength and then he was pumping himself into and out of her, thrusting

ever deeper, seeming to rip her asunder, sinking down and
down . . .

The diplomat started, even though he had been expecting
the mad squeak of the bed and the whore's screams. Harlots
that they were, they always did when the American began
working on them. He was a mad sex beast, who knew no
mercy even when he was supposed to be having pleasure
with these paid women. It was almost as if he got more
pleasure out of cruelty, even torture, than from the sexual
act. But the diplomat knew he couldn't afford to waste
any time on philosophizing about the American's sexual
motivation. If he was going to carry out his plan, he'd better
do it right away while the American was still engaged in
his bedroom.

He turned to Miguel, who was grinning in the corner,
head cocked to one side as he listened to the steady
squeaking of the bedsprings above them. '*A delante, hombre*,' he commanded, 'and take that foolish grin off your
silly face, peasant.'

Miguel did so immediately. Indeed he jumped from his
chair, clicked to attention like the soldier he had once been
and barked, '*A su servicio, Senor.*'

'You know what to do?'

Miguel nodded, still standing rigidly to attention.

'Then stop fooling around and playing soldier. He'll be
finished with her soon and then he'll make his attempt.
Everything has to be in position by then. *A la attaque!*'

That did it. 'To the attack' pleased the ex-soldier. He
saluted incorrectly and rushed out as if he were back on
the Ebro charging the Reds' lines.

The diplomat sat back a moment and took stock of the
situation. The discovery of the knife had been the start of
the affair. At first they thought the knife had been mislaid.

But when they had conducted the morning search of his room, which they did routinely every day when Larsen went to have his shower, and had found it, sharpened like a stiletto, they had known he was up to something. Soon thereafter they had discovered that the tall bedroom window had been forced and when they had spotted his footprints outside on the dusty balustrade they had reasoned he had been outside and was preparing for an escape down the facade of the legation building.

Surprisingly enough it had been that peasant, Miguel, the ex-soldier-cum-watchman, who had come up with the last piece in the jigsaw. 'He will go,' he had declared with the slow dogmatic certainty of the Andalusian peasant which he had once been, 'now he has a woman, *señor.*'

'How do you know?' the diplomat had asked testily.

The watchman had made the Spanish gesture of counting money with his horny, work-hardened thumb and forefinger. 'Because she will have money and he has none, *señor*. Money, he will need to travel and to escape. It is logical.'

The diplomat had realized it was. He realized too that Larsen was playing into his hands. The crazy American had his own plans of escape – to where it didn't matter – but escape he would. Therefore, just as the American would attempt to betray him, he would betray the American – and he would do so *first*. The American would disappear from the face of the earth and that would be that. The diplomat wiped one hand against the other like the peasants did when they wiped the earth from their dirty hands and smiled, suddenly pleased with himself. The problem of what to do with the American pig was solved.

Paula bucked and shook. Her eyes were blind with tears. Weakly she fought to break away from the monster. To no avail. He was far too strong for her. Now he was unbothered by her pathetic resistance. Indeed he seemed totally oblivious of her. His big paws were clamped to her buttocks, pressing his fingers cruelly into the soft flesh, as he rode her harder and harder. He used his erection like a weapon of sadistic anger, smashing her insides without feeling, buried in a world of his own, as if she were not there.

At first she prayed to God that he would simply finish, leave her in peace with her burning hurt. 'God,' she sobbed to herself, 'let him come, *please!*' But God didn't oblige her. He pounded her loins in savage, mindless, heartless lust, as if he would never finish; as if he were unable to finish.

It was then it dawned on her. He *couldn't* finish. He had *never* been able to finish in spite of that massive organ of his of which he was so inordinately proud. She knew what impotent show-offs and boasters were like. Frustrated, unable to please a woman, their vanity hurt immeasurably, they took their revenge on their women, with curses, blows, non-payment of what they had promised at the beginning. But this one was different. This one would take his revenge in the most drastic manner of all – *by murder!*

Now she knew this one would show no mercy. This was a long sexual ride to death. Weakly she sobbed, 'Oh Rory, be quick . . . please . . . he's going to kill me . . . Rory . . .' Larsen continued to pound her battered body . . .

Rory O'Corrigan knew it was time to move now. Paula would have satisfied the bugger. After sex, Larsen would be easier to take. He coughed. The signal for the policeman and the Intelligence wallah, Mackenzie, that he was going in, and eased himself almost noiselessly from the cab. Swiftly, bent double, he crossed to the embassy wall. It presented no problem to O'Corrigan. His Commando training saw to that. He leapt upwards, caught the parapet at his first go, swung himself upwards and in one and the same movement was over and dropped to the ground. He paused there. He turned his head to left and right. Nothing. Still he wasn't satisfied. He didn't want to cock up the job at this late stage. He bent low, and gazed from there. It was an old Commando trick. From that angle, even on the darkest of nights, one could usually make out something. But all he could see were the tailored bushes of the embassy standing there next to the nineteenth-century facade of the big house like silent sentinels. O'Corrigan nodded his approval. Stealthily he moved forward at a crouch. His heart was beating normally. He wasn't even sweating. He was perfectly in control of himself, which was good. The next few minutes were going to be difficult, he knew that.

By now Larsen would be relaxed – he had dismissed the unpleasant, repulsive even, thought of how Paula had achieved that aim. Now Paula would pretend she wanted to go to the lavatory. O'Corrigan didn't know whether Larsen would have a lavatory in his room, but Paula would find some sort of pretext for getting out of bed and crossing to the big window, still carefully blacked out. Once there she'd draw the curtains back and flick on the light switch. Larsen had been in Britain long enough to know just how important it was not to show a light during the blackout. They guessed he'd protest, tell her to put the light out. She'd find some excuse for getting him to do so, but leaving the curtains open. Once he, O'Corrigan, saw the light go out, with the curtains still undrawn, he'd be in, chloroform pad at the ready. Larsen was a big bastard, but the superintendent had assured him that the pad would knock out an ox. Automatically he touched his back pocket to ensure the bottle and the cotton-wool pad were still there.

They were. He took a deep breath and headed for the next step . . .

Miguel paused. He thought he had heard something moving in the grounds. He listened for a moment or two. Nothing, save the gentle hiss of the wind. He shook his head and told himself that as an old soldier he should know that the night and darkness played tricks on a man's imagination. Probably, if anything, it might be one of those stray cats that plagued London these days. Abandoned by their owners at the start of the air raids, they had become feral, living off what they could forage. The little Spanish watchman smiled to himself. Back in the Civil War the cats themselves would have been the forage. Many a time he and his half-starved comrades had made a fine stew out of a dead cat and whatever vegetables they could find in the abandoned gardens of the peasants. He moved on.

Now he could make out the box-like shape of the taxi some fifty metres away down the road running alongside the embassy. It wasn't difficult to see. For it had the regulation white-painted lines along its bumpers and running boards. He started to approach it noiselessly, head cocked to one side to check whether the Englishman who drove it might be awake. But no sound came from the pre-war taxi. He moved on. Slowly, very slowly, he came up to the taxi from the roadside where he would be shielded from anyone hidden in the bushes next to the pavement. He paused again. Still no sound. For a moment the taxi was flooded by the spectral light of the moon. He froze. Still nothing. He might well have been the last man left alive in the world. The moon slid behind the clouds once more. He advanced another few paces. Reaching inside his shabby jacket, he pulled out the bundle carefully. He didn't want to take any chances with it; one false move and he might well be sitting up on a cloud, clothed in white robes and playing his harp with the angels. He grinned at the thought, baring his yellow rotten teeth. He told himself that if anyone would be playing his harp with the angels, it wouldn't be Miguel dos Santos. He prepared to attach the device . . .

At last he was finished with her. She lay there on the rumpled sheet, as if dead. She breathed shallowly like a tortured animal attempting to recover. Larsen had already risen. In the darkness, she could hear him wiping his loins with a towel. She stirred. The bed creaked. She sensed him turning to look down at her in the semi-darkness. 'I must go to the lavatory,' she whispered faintly.

He laughed easily, obviously well pleased with himself. 'I sure knocked the piss out of ya, didn't I?' he said, adding, 'There's no john here. You'll have to use the pisspot under the bed.'

She sat up weakly. 'I can't see.'

'Feel,' he said unthinkingly. 'That is if you've not felt enough already.' He chuckled softly. 'I sure gave it to you, bitch, didn't I just? I bet you'll never have a guy half the equal of me up there ever again, *eh*?' As weak as she was, she noted the underlying threat in that final *eh*? As degraded as she felt, as if her body inside and out was unclean, she remembered she was dealing with a savage killer, whose mood could change at any minute. 'Yes,' she forced herself to say and rose from the bed.

'Fine. Any time you want more of the same, doll, just let me know. You can call the ultimate love machine. Any time.' But even as Larsen said the words, he told himself there would be no next time. The whore was coming out with him as far as the taxi. She'd keep the cab driver busy till he'd gotten their dough and then he'd be off into the wild blue yonder. He hadn't yet decided what to do with both of them. But he'd think of something. First things first. ''Kay, take a piss if you want to,' he said, 'but make it snappy. Then get dressed.'

'Yes,' she replied and began to feel her way to the window and the blackout curtain while he busied himself putting on his clothes. Why, she didn't know or care. All she wanted was to be out of this terrible place, away from the madman and in the safety of Rory's brawny arms.

A dozen or so yards away, Rory O'Corrigan heaved himself up the drainpipe effortlessly. His weeks of hiding in Paula's tight little flat had not weakened him, though he had been unable to go out in the daylight. He felt as fit as he had ever done and the knowledge that Paula was still closeted with that mad killer Larsen lent urgency to his movement. Now he was just beneath the window to the latter's room. Any moment now, she'd pull back the blind, if everything was going to plan. It was. For now he could hear the faint hiss as someone pulled at a curtain cord. It had to be Paula. He tensed, holding on with one hand, ready to reach up instantly with the other and grab for the window sill. A moment later he would have forced the window and clasped the pad around Larsen's mouth and that would be that bar the shouting.

Slowly, with a little squeak, the curtain was drawn back. He didn't look. Instead he kept his head lowered just in case Larsen looked out. He counted off the seconds. Then it happened. The light clicked on. A shaft of yellow light stabbed the darkness. 'What in Sam Hill's name . . . !' came the angry shout in Larsen's voice. 'Cut that fucking light will ya, bitch!'

Paula spat something back and he could tell by her tone that she wasn't herself.

A slap. Paula screamed. O'Corrigan waited no longer.

With a grunt he heaved himself up, knife at the ready to force the window. But that wasn't necessary. Next instant the window opened of its own accord. O'Corrigan was caught off guard. Larsen took in the situation instantly. '*You!*' he yelled furiously. His big fist slammed into O'Corrigan's face brutally. The Irishman was caught off balance. He reeled back, spitting blood. Just in time he managed to hang on and stop himself from falling from his handhold. It was then that he caught the glimpse of silver steel. The American had a knife – and he intended to use it. Hanging there with one hand, feeling sick and groggy from that cruel punch, O'Corrigan realized he had only moments to live. Now Larsen would strike and that would be that. If the knife didn't kill him, the fall probably would. His last moment had come.

# Four

O'Corrigan hadn't reckoned with Paula.

All her adult life, ever since she had lost her virginity at thirteen, Paula had been on the game one way or another. But in her own way she loved the big tough Irishman, though she knew he didn't love her. Now it was her time, she knew that instinctively, to prove her love for him. She'd save him, though in the end, she realized, he would die violently. But not yet.

Stark naked as she was, suddenly finding new strength at the thought of the danger to Rory, she sprang on to the unsuspecting American's back. She caught him completely by surprise. The knife fell out of his hand and clattered to the floor. Like an all-in wrestler, she grabbed him with one hand. With the other she inserted her fingers into his nostrils and tugged hard. Hot blood flowed at once.

Larsen yelped with agony. Madly he swung his massive body from side to side, trying to throw her off. Hating him, she clung on. She tugged harder at his nostrils. She tore the flesh. Blood poured down his chin. He pummelled her naked ribs to no avail. She no longer felt the pain. Her whole being was concentrated on hanging on to his back till Rory rescued her. Gasping with the effort, clamping her bare knees into his side,

199

she choked, 'Now how do you like it, you big American bastard?'

He didn't . . .

Behind the bushes, Mackenzie and the superintendent became aware of the noise. Mackenzie flung up his night glasses and focused them on the killer's bedroom and the surrounding area. Vague images came into view. For someone had turned off the bedroom light. Two people struggling in the window. Below, a man, who could only be O'Corrigan, hanging on desperately with one hand, trying to swing himself back to his hold once more and not doing so very well.

'Look.' He handed the glasses to the superintendent, reaching inside his pocket for the little revolver.

'Christ Almighty!' the policeman gasped. 'O'Corrigan's made a balls-up of it . . .'

'O'Corrigan is going to die,' Mackenzie interrupted angrily, 'if we don't do something about it, Super.'

'But what can we do? It's more than my job's worth to enter neutral territory. The Assistant Commissioner would have me on the carpet straight off. My boots wouldn't touch the ground – and then there's my pension.'

'Fuck your pension!' Mackenzie said cruelly. 'O'Corrigan's going to die,' he repeated, 'if we don't get our finger out and do something. He won't be worrying about pensions.'

Five metres away, Miguel was poised. The diversion suited him 100 per cent. He crossed the few metres to the cab, crouched low. Nothing stirred inside it. He pulled out the magnetic bomb device and activated it. Holding his breath, he bent and slipped it under the engine, where any casual observer wouldn't spot it. There was a slight clanging noise as the powerful magnet stuck. He gave it a slight push with his hand. It didn't move. It was firmly attached. He grinned wolfishly. When it went off the great lover of an *Americano* might survive, but he'd never again dance the mattress polka. He'd have nothing to do it with. It would be the ultimate Latin revenge. The man without balls. '*Adios, hombre*,' he whispered to himself and then he was gone, disappearing silently into the night shadows.

Mackenzie and the superintendent stood there perplexed. Mackenzie understood the policeman's position. But he just couldn't let O'Corrigan die without making the attempt to save him. He made up his mind. 'I'm going over the wall,' he said urgently.

'But you're in uniform. If the Spaniards nab you and our authorities get to know, you're for the high jump, laddie.' But already the young Intelligence officer had gone, running lightly for the wall and what lay beyond.

Larsen stopped struggling and trying to toss her from his back. He bit his bottom lip till the blood came; the agony was too great. All the same he knew he had only seconds left. Soon the spics would hear the commotion and would come running and then that would be that.

Paula was caught off guard. She opened her mouth to tell him not to hit Rory again and in that same instant, Larsen came to life again. He ducked and with a heave of his brutally muscled shoulders sent her flying over his head. She slammed against the wall beneath the window and, already unconscious, slithered down it, her head to one side, her legs wide open as if she were ready for sex yet again.

'Clever cunt,' he said thickly, the coppery-tasting blood trickling down his throat. 'I hope you broke your goddam neck.' He wiped the back of his big hand across his face. He kicked her in the ribs. Her breasts wobbled. But she didn't react otherwise. She was out. 'Serves you right.' He bent and wiped his bloody hand across the breasts. They flushed a dark red. That pleased him. Indeed, he grew excited. He wished he had time. He'd show her – and the world – what happened to bitches like her, who teased and tormented men, laughing behind their backs. Yes, by God, if he only had time he'd ensure that she never would be capable physically of humiliating men ever again.

Suddenly the red mist of lust and cruelty dispersed. He heard movement below. Then he remembered that big Mick swine, O'Corrigan. He was in the way. If he was going to escape this night, he'd have to deal with him. That O'Corrigan was one tough hombre. He knew that from the Commando training camp.

Hastily he picked up the whore's purse. He scrabbled inside and snatched the wad of notes that the spic faggot had given her. He guessed it might be as much as twenty pounds. He stuffed it into his pocket. With his other hand he switched off the tell-tale light. For an instant he paused at the window, blinking his eyes, getting accustomed to the darkness. Slightly below him he heard a sigh. O'Corrigan, the Mick bastard, was coming. There was no time to waste. He had to deal with him. He threw his leg over the window sill, treading unfeelingly on the unconscious Paula. She sighed. He grimaced. Christ, she wasn't dead yet. But there was no time. The Good Lord would have to forgive him on this occasion for not having dealt with her correctly. 'Get on with it, you jerk,' the voice inside his head urged. 'You ain't got all the time in the frigging world, ya know.'

'Yessir,' he answered promptly. 'Sorry, sir . . . I'm on my way.' He pulled his other leg over the sill and saw O'Corrigan balanced there. 'OK,' he said aloud, 'take this—'

Down below in the grounds, Mackenzie heard the angry threat. Instinctively he knew what Larsen was about. He raised his pistol. Even as he did so, he realized what he was going to do was totally wrong. He was already violating neutral territory in army uniform. Even worse, now he was about to use a firearm. They'd cashier him if he were apprehended. Perhaps they might even sentence him to prison, the dreaded 'glasshouse', as they had poor old O'Corrigan, even though he'd won the country's Military Cross for bravery in action. All the same, stupid as his action might be, Mackenzie knew he had to do it. O'Corrigan had suffered enough, unjustly so. Mackenzie told himself he must suffer no more. He deserved better of his adopted country.

He raised the pistol and took aim at the shadowy figure now getting out of the window to deal with the trapped Irishman. He took first pressure, controlling his breathing carefully, as if he were back on the pistol range. Then he squeezed the trigger fully. The pistol jerked upwards. Crack! The muzzle spat scarlet flame. Up above, Larsen yelled. He staggered back against the window, clutching his wounded shoulder. O'Corrigan cried something.

Abruptly all was noise and confusion. Everywhere in the embassy lights flashed on. In an instant the windows which were not blacked out flooded the garden below with their light. There were cries of surprise and alarm. Frantically, half-dressed servants hurried back and forth, pulling curtains, fixing shutters. The watchmen streamed from their room, shouting orders and counter-orders. Out in the street there was the jingling of a police bell as a squad car sped through deserted streets to the scene of the emergency. A warden in a white helmet dashed his bicycle to the ground, shrilled angrily on his whistle and cried, 'Put that bloody light out at once!' And in the midst of it all, Mackenzie stood there, pistol in hand, wondering a little stupidly what he should do next.

Larsen, the ex-Ranger, knew what *he* had to do next. His training clicked in instinctively. He grabbed for the drainpipe. 'Stop there!' O'Corrigan cried weakly. Larsen aimed a kick at his face. He missed. He cursed and forgot the big Mick. The blood was jetting from his shoulder wound and he knew he had to get to the taxi below and be off before he weakened too much and fell into their hands.

Swiftly, using only his powerful legs and his unwounded arm, he descended the pipe. He dropped lightly to the ground. He caught sight of the man who had fired at him. He dodged into the shrubbery just as Mackenzie spotted him, too. 'Halt!' Mackenzie cried, but Larsen was not stopping for anyone or anything. Up front one of the watchmen was opening the gate. Larsen knew it was the opportunity he was waiting for, then he didn't feel he had the strength to tackle the wall. He darted forward, as Mackenzie spotted him again, raised his pistol and then lowered it a little helplessly. He daren't fire now; there were too many civilians streaming into the grounds, crying wildly, '*Ladrón . . . Hay ladrón . . . !*' Now he had to get O'Corrigan out. The Spaniards would take care of Paula, he was sure.

Larsen bit his lip, trying to suppress the burning pain in his wounded shoulder. The watchman, opening the heavy gate with the arms of Spain decorating it, was too busy with his task. So far he had not heard Larsen. The big Ranger didn't give him a chance to do so. He summoned up all his remaining strength and darted from the bushes. Even as the watchman, hearing the noise, had begun turning, Larsen was on him. His good arm went round the startled Spaniard's throat. In that same instant, Larsen thrust his knee into the small of the watchman's back. He pulled and thrust in one violent movement. The watchman's tongue shot out. He gurgled. A click and suddenly he went limp in Larsen's grip. His spinal cord had been snapped. Like two desperate lovers they clung together for a moment. Larsen's nostrils were full of the unconscious man's smell: a mixture of cheap black cigarettes and garlic. Then, with a gesture of disgust, he dropped the watchman in a crumpled motionless heap, was through the gate and sprinting almost noiselessly towards the taxi.

He flung a glance inside. No sign of the driver. Larsen reasoned hastily he'd gone to take a piss somewhere in the bushes. It didn't matter. He could see the key stuck in the ignition. He knew that drivers were supposed to immobilize their vehicles when they left them. But he guessed that like most drivers, the missing taxi driver would have been too lazy to do so. Anyway he'd soon find out whether the driver had taken the carburettor with him. Grimacing with the pain of his arm, but knowing he was going to overcome it – he'd apply some first aid, once he was safely out of London – he slid behind the wheel.

Somewhere someone blew a whistle. A voice cried, 'Hold it there!' Larsen paid no heed. He turned the key. There was the hoarse whirr of the starter. But the motor didn't start. 'Holy cow!' Larsen cried in sudden rage. There was the sound of feet pounding down the blacked-out road in his direction. Someone was running out of the nearby legation, panting, 'Stop . . . now . . . or I'll fire, d'you hear!'

'Fuck you!' Larsen yelled back, concentrating on the motor. Suddenly sweat was pouring down his contorted face. He turned the key again. The burr was louder. 'Come on . . . *start!*' he raged. The feet were coming closer. The man at the gate had crouched and raised his pistol. Madly Larsen worked the key. He knew he had only seconds left.

Mackenzie fired. And missed. The slug howled off the ARP static water main. He cursed and pressed the trigger again. Nothing! The little pistol had jammed. Hastily, hand trembling with tension, he ejected the cartridge. Across the road the sound of the ancient taxi beginning to start up became louder and louder. He took aim and began to squeeze the trigger as he had been taught, his foresight neatly dissecting Larsen's blond head in the moonlight which had now appeared through the clouds. 'All right, you swine—' he began.

Too late! The old motor burst into life with a roar. Larsen didn't hesitate. He thrust home the taxi's first gear. It moved forward with a great jolt. Hastily he double-declutched into second gear in the same moment that the bullet shattered the rear window. Larsen laughed uproariously. He'd done it. He'd fooled the bastards. He'd escaped. He was on his way back to the good ole US of A. *'So long, suckers!'* he yelled to no one in particular, and then he was gone, driving without lights, disappearing into the darkness of a blacked out wartime London . . .

The explosion caught him totally by surprise. Fifteen minutes previously he had stopped, just as the blood-red ball to the east indicated that it was almost dawn, and patched up the wound the best he could. At least the bleeding had ceased and in that blood-red light he could see he had been lucky. The bullet hadn't penetrated the bone as he had feared, though it hurt like hell. Still, he could live with it till he could get patched up properly. He had lit one of the missing driver's Woodbines and set off again, heading west to the port from which he would sail for home.

Despite his pain, Larsen felt happy. He had fooled them all and he had carried out the Good Lord's work to rid the world of women who flaunted themselves, led men into temptation and then laughed scornfully when those men were unable to do what these lustful women desired of them. Oh yes, when his time came he knew the Good Lord would have a place waiting for him up there in His Kingdom.

Suddenly, surprisingly, just as he had changed down to take the road which led into Reading, the taxi heaved. In that second before he realized – too late – what was happening, he thought he'd had a blowout. 'Darnit!' he began, as, frighteningly, the taxi rose beneath him. '*Nooooo*—' he begged. His scream of fear and pain was lost in the earsplitting blast of the time bomb exploding. Red flame shot up before his eyes.

Beneath him the floor of the vehicle disintegrated in the same instant that he lost control, smashing into the stone wall opposite. Then he was dead and there was silence.

Half an hour later a military policeman on a motorcycle marking the way for the follow-up convoy came across the wrecked car and the remains of Larsen's body. Its bottom half had been ripped open. All around the corpse on the blackened scorched road, there were the shreds of Larsen's meat and bones, the ruptured guts oozing out the contents of his shattered stomach, the mangled sausage which had once been the penis that he had been so proud of.

The redcap had seen some horrible things in his time. But never anything like this. The bile rose in his throat. He fought off the need to be sick. '*God, does he stink!*' he growled thickly, holding his nose in horrified disgust. Then the stench took hold of him. He couldn't control himself. He started to vomit, shoulders heaving violently with the effort, the hot steaming spew drenching what was left of that horrible body . . .

# Envoi

'They were men rudely torn away from the joys of life. Like any other men whom you take in the mass, they were ignorant and of narrow outlook, full of sound common sense, disposed to be led and do as they were bid, enduring under hardship and suffering . . . but at intervals there were cries and dark shudders of humanity that issued from the silence and the shadows of great human hearts.'

*Henri Barbuse. WWI*

'*They say there's a troopship . . . bound for old Blighty's shore . . . heavily laden with time-expired men, bound for the land they adore . . . They're saying good-bye to them all, the long and the short and the tall . . . So fuck 'em all, as back to their billets they crawl . . . You'll get no promotion this side of the ocean, so cheer up my lads, fuck 'em all . . .*' Lustily the men of the 'Battleaxe' division sang the ribald ditty while the military band played merrily and file after file of heavily laden infantry, helmets and forage caps cocked to one side, struggled up the gangplanks to disappear into the bowels of the great troopship.

Officials moved back and forth, checking their boards self-importantly. Bored sailors, caps at the backs of their heads, half-smoked cigarettes tucked away behind their ears, worked on the derricks. Naval officers barked orders. Sergeant-majors, pacing sticks tucked rigidly beneath their right arms, marched up and down the quay, crying, 'Get a move on there, lads! The war won't wait for ever, yer know. Now come on there, you bunch o' pregnant penguins, a bit sharpish now . . .'

Leaning against a derrick, smoking silently, waiting for his company to be ordered to embark, Lieutenant Rory O'Corrigan, the black armband for poor dead Paula still around his khaki sleeve, told himself he had seen it all so often before: the bold, the fearful, the show-offs, the

211

reluctant heroes, the many different types that went to make up an infantry battalion. *Full of piss and vinegar*, a little voice at the back of his head commented cynically, *at present. But what will they be like when the shite starts flying?* He could guess, when half a company could vanish in an hour, dead and dying in a khaki carpet across some bloody hillside, the very name of which they didn't even know when they attacked; and if they did, those who survived it would have forgotten by the time they tackled the next hill. He took a drag at his pipe and dismissed the morbid thought. In war, he told himself philosophically, it was wise not to think of the future, but to live for the present: it was the only way to prevent yourself from going mad.

Suddenly he straightened up and took the pipe out of his mouth. A familiar figure was pushing his way through the crowded quayside making straight towards him. It was young Mackenzie, who had done so much to help him and had been a tower of strength at his second court martial and after Paula's slow death. The young officer recognized him. A smile banished his serious look. Rory O'Corrigan smiled too as he noticed that this particular member of the 'green slime' was doing very well for himself; he had been promoted yet again. He came to the position of attention and saluted smartly. 'Good to see you, sir,' he said. 'May I congratulate you on your promotion, *Captain* Mackenzie.'

Mackenzie mouthed, 'Fuck you,' and stretched out his hand. 'Good to see you again. Thought I'd pop down to Tilbury and see you off to – er – foreign parts.'

'Rank hath its privileges.' He relaxed. 'Good to see you, too. Glad you could come. Bit lonely these days without you – well, you know. May a humble second lieutenant shake the hand of a captain?'

'You may, you cheeky bugger,' Mackenzie answered. He looked up at the decks of the big troopship crowded with the infantry of the 76th Division. 'Your men look in fine fettle, Rory.'

'They're lads really. Not as well trained as the Commandos. But they'll try and, in the end, I suppose they'll be good soldiers – those who survive.'

Mackenzie frowned, but said nothing. For suddenly an icy finger of apprehension had traced its way slowly down his spine. For at that moment, with the surety of a vision, he knew he'd never see O'Corrigan again. The big, tough Irishman was fated never to return to 'Old Blighty's Shore', and Mackenzie guessed he knew it at that moment.

Thus they parted. Half an hour later the big trooper disappeared into the autumn gloom. On the quayside the military band still played, although the place was deserted now. Even the dockers had gone. In latter years Mackenzie seemed to recall that it was one of those Gracie Fields songs that they played on such occasions – 'Wish Me Luck As I Wave You Goodbye' perhaps.

But to his mind that bold defiant chorus those young men of the 'Battleaxe Division' had thundered before they had left Tilbury, with its fatalistic, bolshy chant of 'Fuck 'em all!' seemed to symbolize their departure. '*So you'll get no promotion this side of the ocean, so cheer up my lads, fuck 'em all . . .*'

# Author's Note

Acting Major R. O'Corrigan, MC was killed in action leading his company in an attack in the Primosole Bridge area in the summer of 1943. For that brave attack in that long forgotten blazingly hot summer in Sicily, he was recommended for the country's highest honour, the Victoria Cross. It was never awarded due to his previous bad military record. They say he's buried somewhere in Sicily – unfortunately I can't say exactly where, but I know he's there somewhere.

*L.K.*